用最有效率的方法在最短時間內

記憶更多英文單字的秘密！

使用說明

學習小撇步 1

系統化分類方便查找

對於想要把這本書當作工具書查找的讀者們，可以參考目錄搭配使用。在書中，我們將大分類化成三個章節，分別是：字首、字根、字尾，再往下的分類是每個章節中由功能或使用時機點劃分而成，比如「數量」、「方向」等，採用功能式的分類比起使用字母順序編排更方便使用者需要尋找特定情境中可以用的字根X字首X字尾，另一方面，在複習的時候也會更加容易。

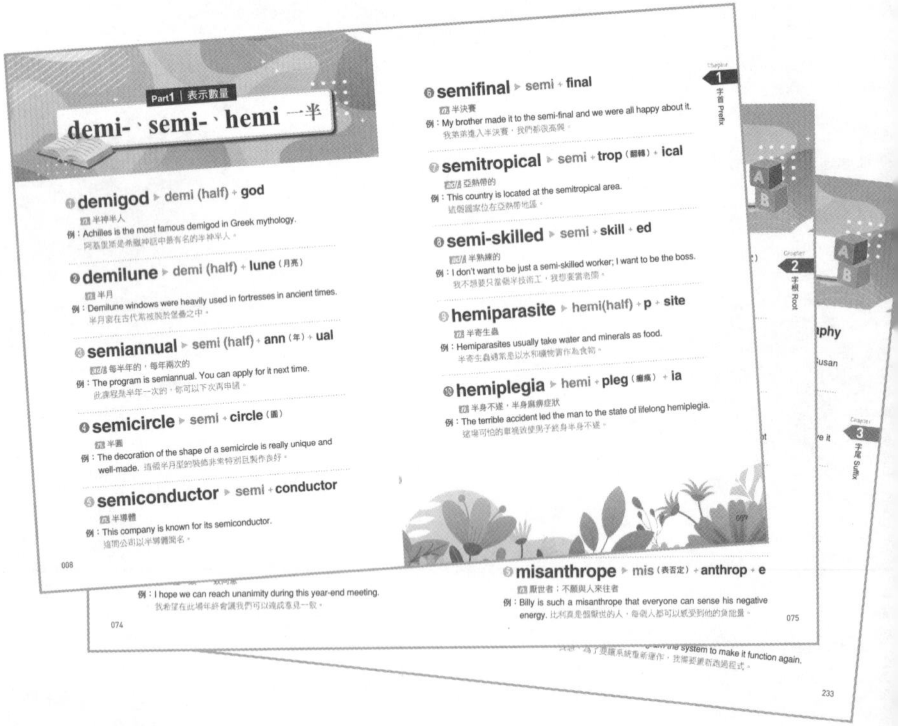

Part1｜表示數量

demi-、semi-、hemi 一半

❶ **demigod** ▸ demi (half) + god
名 半神半人
例：Achilles is the most famous demigod in Greek mythology.
阿基里斯是希臘神話中最有名的半神半人。

❷ **demilune** ▸ demi (half) + lune (月亮)
名 半月
例：Demilune windows were heavily used in fortresses in ancient times.
半月窗在古代常被用於堡壘之中。

❸ **semiannual** ▸ semi (half) + ann (年) + ual
形/名 每半年的，每年兩次的
例：The program is semiannual. You can apply for it next time.
此課程是半年一次的，你可以下次再申請。

❹ **semicircle** ▸ semi + circle (圓)
名 半圓
例：The decoration of the shape of a semicircle is really unique and well-made. 這個半月型的裝飾非常特別且製作良好。

❺ **semiconductor** ▸ semi + conductor
名 半導體
例：This company is known for its semiconductor.
這間公司以半導體聞名。

008

❻ **semifinal** ▸ semi + final
名 半決賽
例：My brother made it to the semi-final and we were all happy about it.
我弟弟進入半決賽，我們都很高興。

❼ **semitropical** ▸ semi + trop (翻轉) + ical
形/名 亞熱帶的
例：This country is located at the semitropical area.
這個國家位在亞熱帶地區。

❽ **semi-skilled** ▸ semi + skill + ed
形/名 半熟練的
例：I don't want to be just a semi-skilled worker; I want to be the boss.
我不想要只當個半技術工，我想要當老闆。

❾ **hemiparasite** ▸ hemi(half) + p + site
名 半寄生蟲
例：Hemiparasites usually take water and minerals as food.
半寄生蟲通常是以水和礦物質作為食物。

❿ **hemiplegia** ▸ hemi + pleg (癱瘓) + ia
名 半身不遂，半身麻痺症狀
例：The terrible accident led the man to the state of lifelong hemiplegia.
這場可怕的車禍致使男子終身半身不遂。

Chapter 1 字首 Prefix

009

例：I hope we can reach unanimity during this year-end meeting.
我希望在此場年終會議我們可以達成意見一致。

074

❺ **misanthrope** ▸ mis (表否定) + anthrop + e
名 厭世者；不願與人來往者
例：Billy is such a misanthrope that everyone can sense his negative energy. 比利真是個厭世的人，每個人都可以感受到他的負能量。

075

Chapter 2 字根 Root

Chapter 3 字尾 Suffix

...the system to make it function again.
...為了要讓系統重新運作，我需要重新過程式。

233

學習小撇步 2

拆解單字，從字源理解記憶

其實英文單字不需要死背，單字基本上是由字根 (root)、字首 (prefix)、字尾 (suffix) 所組成，被拆解後的英文單字中，其組成結構有些和希臘文、拉丁文或其他歐系語言有關聯，只要記得字源的意思，就可以擺脱硬記死背，從「理解」的層面去學習單字，在此，書中每個單字都附上其拆解後的結構組成，並適時補充説明字源的涵義，以加強學習的深度。

學習小撇步 3

中英對照例句，學習成果更深而廣

除了列出每個字源的選字以外，每個單字都附有一個精心編寫的中英文對照例句、詞性和中文意義，讓讀者在學習字根 X 字首 X 字尾時，還能從例句中兼顧英文學習的單字應用、寫作、會話層面。

學習小撇步 4

可以拆解並猜測陌生單字意思的秘密

這本書就像一本字根 X 字首 X 字尾用法的「入門説明使用書」，記憶書中所列舉的字根 X 字首 X 字尾，就像獲得一把能夠開啟許多道門的鑰匙，往後在遇到沒有看過的生字時，只要會拆解其架構、而且碰到記憶過的字源，就算是生字，也能猜測其意思，比起硬背單字，使用這個方法來學習英文單字相對的會大幅提升效率。

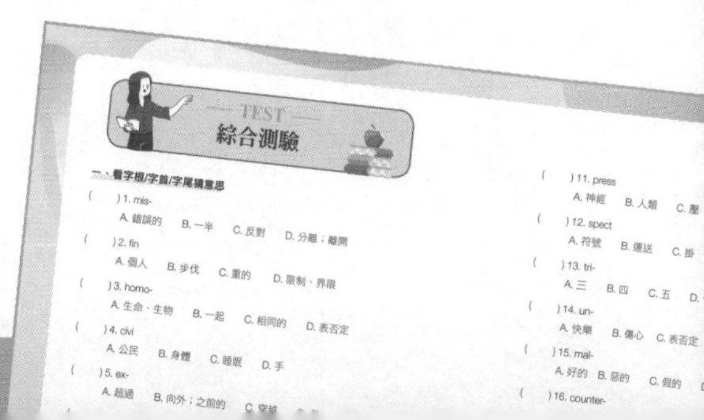
— TEST —
綜合測驗

一、看字根/字首/字尾猜意思

( ) 1. mis-
A. 錯誤的 B. 一半 C. 反對 D. 分離；離開

( ) 2. fin
A. 個人 B. 步伐 C. 重的 D. 限制、界限

( ) 3. homo-
A. 生命、生物 B. 一起 C. 相同的 D. 表否定

( ) 4. civi
A. 公民 B. 身體 C. 睡眠 D. 手

( ) 5. ex-
A. 超過 B. 向外；之前的 C.

( ) 11. press
A. 神經 B. 人類 C. 壓

( ) 12. spect
A. 符號 B. 運送 C. 掛

( ) 13. tri-
A. 三 B. 四 C. 五 D. 十

( ) 14. un-
A. 快樂 B. 傷心 C. 表否定

( ) 15. mal-
A. 好的 B. 惡的 C. 假的 D.

( ) 16. counter-

前言

台灣人學了十幾年的英文，英文程度在亞洲中卻不及許多國家，常聽許多人抱怨：單字量不夠、文法太難、對口說缺乏自信⋯⋯，語言基礎要打好的話，單字量是不可或缺的，不過，學習單字時一定要用死背的方式土法煉鋼嗎？其實可以使用「字根、字首、字尾」來幫助學習喔！

就像中文字中有「部首」，英文單字也可以被拆解，被拆解成的部分就可以分成「字根、字首、字尾」，這些字源的來源廣泛，古希臘、拉丁文等等，比起一個單字一個單字硬記，記憶字源等於是記憶了語言的「造字法」，引導大家從最根本的字源層面去學習英文，而既然單字都是由字根、字首、字尾所組成，直接學習字根、字首、字尾就會比背誦單字更有效率，拿來歸納、整理單字時很方便，在遇到生字時也會因為看過相同的字源而能夠輕鬆猜出單字意思。

學習的方法千百種，只要找到適合自己的方式、能靈活運用，就可以被稱作好方法。背單字的過程很乏味，想要有效率記憶更多單字，關鍵在於瞭解單字的結構。學習的路上沒有捷徑，但是好的方法能夠幫助我們在過程中少走一些冤枉路，因此，在這裡我們提供了一個能夠幫助大家有效率學習英文單字的方法，請大家務必好好學習！

目錄

Chapter 1

字首 *Prefix*

demi-、semi-、hemi 一半

❶ demigod ▸ demi (half) + god

n. 半神半人

例：Achilles is the most famous demigod in Greek mythology.
阿基里斯是希臘神話中最有名的半神半人。

❷ demilune ▸ demi (half) + lune（月亮）

n. 半月

例：Demilune windows were heavily used in fortresses in ancient times.
半月窗在古代常被裝於堡壘之中。

❸ semiannual ▸ semi (half) + ann（年）+ ual

adj. 每半年的，每年兩次的

例：The program is semiannual. You can apply for it next time.
此課程是半年一次的，你可以下次再申請。

❹ semicircle ▸ semi + circle（圓）

n. 半圓

例：The decoration of the shape of a semicircle is really unique and well-made. 這個半月型的裝飾非常特別且製作良好。

❺ semiconductor ▸ semi + conductor

n. 半導體

例：This company is known for its semiconductor.
這間公司以半導體聞名。

❻ semifinal ▶ semi + final

n. 半決賽

例：My brother made it to the semi-final and we were all happy about it.
我弟弟進入半決賽，我們都很高興。

❼ semitropical ▶ semi + trop（翻轉）+ ical

adj. 亞熱帶的

例：This country is located at the semitropical area.
這個國家位在亞熱帶地區。

❽ semi-skilled ▶ semi + skill + ed

adj. 半熟練的

例：I don't want to be just a semi-skilled worker; I want to be the boss.
我不想要只當個半技術工，我想要當老闆。

❾ hemiparasite ▶ hemi(half) + p + site

n. 半寄生蟲

例：Hemiparasites usually take water and minerals as food.
半寄生蟲通常是以水和礦物質作為食物。

❿ hemiplegia ▶ hemi + pleg（癱瘓） + ia

n. 半身不遂，半身麻痹症狀

例：The terrible accident led the man to the state of lifelong hemiplegia.
這場可怕的車禍致使男子終身半身不遂。

Part1｜表示數量

mono-、sol-、uni- 單一；一個

❶ monarchy ▸ mon(o) + archy（統治）

n. 君主政治

例：Monarchy is one form of the many government models.
君主政治是眾多治理模式的其中一種。

❷ monogamy ▸ mono + gamy（婚姻）

n. 一夫一妻制

例：Monogamy is performed in most of the countries.
大多數國家皆採取一夫一妻制。

❸ monotony ▸ mono + tony（聲音）

n. 單調的語調，單調乏味

例：I disliked the monotony of the play. It bored me.
我討厭這齣戲的單調乏味。我覺得很無聊。

❹ sole ▸ sol(one) + e

adj. 單獨的，獨佔的

例：Sole agreement from one side isn't enough to execute this contract.
要執行這份合約不能只有單方同意。

❺ solitary ▸ sol(one) + itary

adj. 孤獨的，孤單的，唯一的

例：The man lived a solitary life in the countryside.
男子在鄉間度過孤獨的一生。

❻ solidify ▸ sol + id + ify（動詞字尾）

v. 使團結，使凝固

例：The molten metal solidified and became as hard as a rock.
融化金屬凝固了起來，變得像石頭一樣硬。

❼ unanimity ▸ uni(one) + anim（精神）+ ity

n. 同意，全體一致

例：The discussion finally reached unanimity.
討論終於達成全體同意。

❽ unify ▸ uni(one) + fy(make)

v. 綜合，統一，使一體化

例：I think you should unify these items together before you proceed to the next phase.
在進入下一個階段前，我覺得你應該先把這些項目統一在一起。

❾ uniform ▸ uni + form（形式）

adj. 相同的；一致的 n. 制服

例：Students are required to wear uniform to school.
學生被要求上學要穿制服。

❿ unity ▸ uni + ty（名詞字尾）

n. 統一，和諧

例：To live in unity with other countries is to contribute to world peace.
與他國相處融洽就是對世界和平做出貢獻。

Part1｜表示數量

bi-、di-、duo- 兩個；雙

❶ biannual ▸ bi(two) + annu(year) + al

adj. 一年兩次的，每半年的

例：The seminar is biannual. Don't miss out on it.
此研討會每兩年舉行一次。別錯過。

❷ bicycle ▸ bi + cycle（圓；環）

n. 自行車

例：Let's go ride bicycle along the shore.
我們沿著海岸騎腳踏車吧。

❸ bilateral ▸ bi + later(side) + al

adj. 兩側的，雙邊的

例：This contract requires bilateral agreement.
這份合約需要雙方同意。

❹ bilingual ▸ bi + lingu（語言）+ al

adj. 能說兩種語言的

例：Do you now that both Amy and Adam are bilingual?
你知道艾咪和亞當兩個人都會說兩種語言嗎？

❺ bipartisan ▸ bi + part（部分）+ i + san

adj. 兩黨的

例：Bipartisan approval has been granted to the amendment.
修正案已得到兩黨同意。

❻ bisect ▶ bi + sect（切 = cut）

v. 把……一分為二

例：The doctor bisected the corpse first. 醫生先將屍體一分為二。

❼ dichotomy ▶ dicho(two) + tomy（切 = cut）

adj. 分裂，兩分法，對分

例：Traditional dichotomy of body and soul is questioned now.
傳統的身心二分法現今已遭受質疑。

❽ dilemma ▶ di + lemma（前提）

n. 進退兩難，困局

例：We're all trapped in this moral dilemma. 我們都被困在這個道德難題中了。

❾ dioxide ▶ di + ox(acid) + ide

n. 二氧化物

例：The technicians employ dioxide to create many new materials.
技術員應用二氧化物製造出許多新材料。

❿ duet ▶ du(two) + et

n. 二重唱，二重奏

例：The duet performed in the hall tonight is really worth re-watching.
今晚在宴廳裡表演的二重奏真的值得再次聆聽。

⓫ duplicate ▶ du + plic(fold) + ate

adj. 雙重的，複印的 n. 副本；複印

例：Remember to make a duplicate of this file. 記得將這份檔案留一份副本。

Part1 | 表示數量

tri- 三；quad-、tetra- 四；penta-、quint 五；sexa- 六

❶ triangle ▶ tri + angle（角）n. 三角形

例：The clock in a triangle shape caught my eyes.
三角形的時鐘吸引了我的注意。

❷ trichord ▶ tri + chord(heart)

n. 三弦樂，三弦琴（等）

例：Have you ever heard the sound of a trichord?
你有聽過三弦琴的聲音嗎？

❸ triple ▶ tri + ple（重疊）

adj. 三倍的 v. 使成三倍 n. 三倍數量（的物品）

例：Triple three and you will get nine. 將三乘以三你就會得到九。

❹ quadruple ▶ quadru + ple（重疊）

adj. 四倍的 v. 使成四倍 n. 四倍數量（的物品）

例：I want you to quadruple the sales by the end of the year or you will be fired. 我希望你在年底之前將銷量達到四倍，否則你會被開除。

❺ tetralogy ▶ tetra + logy(speech) n. 四部曲

例：The tetralogy on the apocalypse is well-received by the public.
這部關於世界末日的四部曲廣受大眾好評。

❻ quintuple ▸ quintu + ple

adj. 五倍的 v. 使成五倍 n. 五倍數量（的物品）

例：I can quintuple the sales, not just quadruple. Trust me.
不只四倍，我可以達成五倍銷量。相信我。

❼ pentagon ▸ penta + gon（角）

n. 五角形

例：Pentagon is a landmark building in the United States.
五角大廈是美國著名地標。

❽ pentameter ▸ penta + meter

n. 五步格詩

例：Iambic pentameter is a formed heavily used by William Shakespeare.
抑揚格五步音是威廉莎士比亞常用的格律。

❾ sextuple ▸ sextu + ple（重疊）

adj. 六倍的 v. 使成六倍 n. 六倍數量（的物品）

例：Have you heard that the new sales representative sextuple the sales in one month?
你聽說新來的業務代表在一個月之內將銷售達到六倍？

❿ hexapod ▸ hexa + pod(foot)

v. 六節足動物 adj. 六腳的

例：Hexapod robots are in trend now.
六足機器人現在正流行。

Part1｜表示數量

septa-、hepta- 七；oct- 八；nona- 九；deca-、deci- 十

❶ September ▸ septem(seven) + ber

n. 九月

例：Schools often start in September.
學校大多九月開學。

❷ heptachord ▸ hepta(seven) + chord(heart)

n. 七弦琴，七音音階

例：The band uses heptachord to enhance the overall sound experience.
樂團使用七弦琴來加強整體聽覺體驗。

❸ octagon ▸ octa + gon(angle)

n. 八邊形，八角形

例：The new architecture is built in reference to an ancient octagon memorial hall.
新建築是以一座古老的八角形紀念館做為參考。

❹ octave ▸ oct + ave

n. 八個一組的事物，八度音階 adj. 八個一組的

例：The octave sung by the vocalist is surely beautiful.
那位演唱者唱的八度音階確實很動聽。

❺ octopus ▶ octo + pus(foot)

n. 八爪魚；章魚

例：My dad caught an octopus when fishing today.
我爸爸今天去釣魚時抓到了一隻章魚。

❻ nonary ▶ nona(nine) + ry

n. 九個一組；九進制法 adj. 九進位法的

例：To complete the code, you'll need a nonary scale.
你需要九進位法準則才能完成這個程式。

❼ nonagon ▶ nona + gon(angle)

n. 九邊形

例：See the nonagon building over there? It's the new sports center in our town.
看到那邊的九邊形建築了嗎？它是我們鎮上的新運動中心。

❽ decade ▶ deca(ten) + (a)de

n. 十年

例：Over the last few decades, things have gone entirely different now.
過去幾十年下來，事情已經完全不同了。

❾ decapod ▶ deca + pod(foot)

n. 十足動物 adj. 十足的

例：Decapods scares me more than spiders do.
我害怕十足動物，勝過蜘蛛。

Part1｜表示數量

cent-、hecto- 百；milli-、kilo- 千

❶ century ▸ cent + ury

n. 一百年；世紀

例：The new century is at the corner. It's not the end of the world yet!
新的世紀要到來了。還沒有世界末日！

❷ centimeter ▸ centi + (meter)

n. 釐米；公分

例：You should measure the height and width in centimeters.
你應該要以公分來測量高度和寬度。

❸ centipede ▸ centi + pede(foot)

n. 蜈蚣（源自其擁有100隻腳）

例：Hundreds of centipedes appeared on the road this morning.
上百隻蜈蚣今天早上出現在馬路上。

❹ hectare ▸ hect + are

n. 公頃

例：The farmland stretches to almost seven hectares.
這座農地延伸至幾乎七公頃。

❺ hecatomb ▸ heca + tomb

n. 大屠殺

例：The hecatomb was claimed to take place three centuries ago.
這場大屠殺據說是在三百年前發生的。

❻ millenarian ▸ mill + enar(year) + ian

adj. 一千年的 n. 相信千年盛世的人

例：Millenarians basically misinterpret the prophecies in the Bible.
相信千年盛世的人基本上錯誤理解了聖經裡的預言。

❼ millibar ▸ milli + bar(pressure)

n.（氣壓單位）毫巴

例：This experiment should be conducted using millibar as the parameter. 這場實驗應以毫巴作為實施基準。

❽ kilometer ▸ kilo + meter

n. 一千公尺＝一公里

例：Run for a kilometer first before we begin the drill.
開始鍛鍊之前，先跑一千公尺。

❾ kilogram ▸ kilo + gram

n. 一千公克＝一公斤

例：The bag of rice weighs over five kilograms. 這包米重達超過五公斤。

❿ kilowatt ▸ kilo + watt

n. 千瓦

例：Are you sure the number of kilowatt labeled on the package is correct? 你確定包裝上標示的千瓦數字是正確的嗎？

Part1 | 表示數量

poly-、multi- 多的；pan-、omni- 全部的

❶ polygon ▶ poly + gon（角度）

n. 多角形

例：The new model is specifically made in the shape of a polygon.
新模型特別以多角形的方式進行製作。

❷ polymorphic ▶ poly + morph(form) + ic

adj. 多形態的

例：This new-found element is polymorph and can be applied in many fields. 這個新發現的元素成多型態，且能運用至許多領域。

❸ multiply ▶ multi + ply(fold)

v. （成倍地）增加，乘，繁殖

例：9 multiplies 9 equals 81. 九乘九等於八十一。

❹ multitude ▶ multi + tude（狀態，名詞字尾）

n. 許多，群眾

例：A multitude of issues arise from the disease control this time.
在此次的防疫中，許多問題開始出現。

❺ multi-functional

▶ multi(many) + function（功能） + al

adj. 多功能的

例：This new refrigerator is multi-functional and you should buy it.
這台新冰箱是多功能的，你應該要買。

❻ pandemic ▶ pan(all) + dem(people) + ic

adj. 全國流行的，普遍的 n. 流行病

例：The disease is pandemic. We all should look out for one another.
這是全國流行性疾病。我們應該關照他人。

❼ panorama ▶ pan + orama(look)

n. 全景

例：The panorama of this city is simply stunning.
這座城市的全景簡直就是驚為天人。

❽ omnibus ▶ omni(all) + bus

n. 公車；選集，文集

例：Let's get on the omnibus and explore the city! 搭上公車探索城市吧！

❾ omniscient ▶ omni(all) + sci(know) + ent

adj. 無所不知的，全知的

例：No one is omniscient; we all should humble.
沒有人是全知的，我們都應該謙虛。

❿ omnipresent ▶ omni(all) + present（在場的）

adj. 無所不在的；遍及各處的

例：For Christianity, God is omnipresent. 對基督教來説，上帝是無所不在的。

⓫ omnipotent ▶ omni(all) + potent(powerful)

adj. 全能的；有無限權力（或力量）的

例：Being a president of a country doesn't mean he/ she is omnipresent.
當上國家元首並不泰代表他/她擁有無上權力。

⓬ omnivorous ▶ omni(all) + vor(eat) + ous

adj. 無所不吃的；雜食的

例：Human beings are omnivorous animals. 人類是雜食性動物。

Part2｜表示方向

en-（使）進入

❶ embed ▸ em(put into) + bed

v. 把……牢牢地嵌入、插入、埋入，栽種

例：The little boy embeds the chips into the wooden gadget.
小男孩把晶片放進木製器具裡。

❷ embody ▸ em(put into) + body（身體）

v. 體現，使具體化

例：This painting truly embodies the spirit of Renaissance.
這幅畫真的體現了文藝復興時期的精神。

❸ enroll ▸ en(put into) + roll

v. 登記，註冊

例：Remember to enroll the class by the end of the month.
記得要在月底前選課。

❹ enable ▸ en(make) + able（可以的）

v. 使能夠

例：This equipment further enables me to complete the work faster.
這個設備讓我能夠更加快速的完成工作。

❺ endear ▸ en(make) + dear（心愛）

v. 使人喜愛

例：His generosity endeared everyone at present.
他的慷慨廣受在場的各位喜愛。

⑥ enlarge ▶ en(make) + large（大的）

v. 擴大，詳述

例：I think we should enlarge the photo just a little bit.
我覺得我們應該稍微放大這張照片。

⑦ enrich ▶ en(make) + rich（富有的）

v. 使富有，使豐富

例：This course enriches the diversity of the program.
這堂課使此教學課程的多元性變得更豐富了。

⑧ ensure ▶ en(make) + sure（確定的）

v. 使安全，保證

例：You need to ensure that everyone is evacuated before the fire gets bigger.
在火勢變大之前，你必須確保所有人都已撤離。

⑨ enlighten ▶ en(make) + light（輕的） + en（動詞字尾）

v. 啟發，教育，教導

例：Her teaching enlightened me on a spiritual level.
她的教導在精神層次上啟蒙了我。

⑩ enliven ▶ en(make) + live + (e)n

v. 使有生氣，使活躍

例：The joke suddenly enlivens the atmosphere in the class.
笑話頓時讓整個班的氣氛輕鬆了起來。

Part2 | 表示方向

fore-
前，在前，提前，首先

❶ forearm ▸ fore(front) + arm

n. 前臂

例：The man wears several metal rings on his forearms.
男子在前臂上帶了許多金屬環。

❷ forebode ▸ fore(front) + bode(omen)

v. 預示，預告（=prophesy）

例：There's no use foreboding what to come in the future.
預測未來將會發生何事是沒有用的。

❸ forecast ▸ fore(front) + cast（扔）

n./v. 預測

例：The bureau forecasted that a storm may grow in the next couple of days. 當局預測，暴風將在接下來幾天增長。

❹ foreground ▸ fore(front) + ground（土地）

n.（風景、圖畫的）前景

例：The foreground of this oil painting was set at a rural town.
這幅油畫的前景設定在一座小農村莊。

❺ forehead ▸ fore(front) + head

n. 前額

例：He has a scar on his forehead. 他的額頭有一道傷痕。

❻ foremost ▶ fore(front) + most（最）

n. 第一的，最前的，最重要的

例：First and foremost, you should wash your hand before you eat.
首先，最重要的是你要在吃東西前洗手。

❼ foresee ▶ fore(front) + see（看）

v. 預見，預知

例：The psychic foresaw an incoming tornado.
靈媒預知到有個颶風即將要來。

❽ foretell ▶ fore(front) + tell（說）

v. 預言

例：The witch foretold that the end of the world was coming.
女巫預言世界末日將要到來。

❾ foreword ▶ fore(front) + word（話）

n. 序言，緒論，前言

例：The foreword of this book is really well-written and touching.
這本書的前言寫得真的很好而且感人。

❿ forethought ▶ fore(first) + thought（想法）

n. 事先的考慮，先見

例：Were you to have forethought to do this beforehand, you wouldn't get to this situation.
如果你有事先想到要做這件事，你就不會落到這種下場。

Part2｜表示方向

ante-、anti-、pre- 在……之前

❶ anterior ▸ ante + rior

adj. 前面的，在前的，以前的

例：We surely don't want to go through the period anterior to the war.
我們當然不想要經歷戰前的時代。

❷ ante meridiem ▸ ante + meridiem(noon)

n. 上午（▲in the morning），縮寫為a.m.

例：Be sure to arrive at the venue at 10 ante meridiem.
請確保在早上十點抵達會場。

❸ antechamber ▸ ante + chamber

n. 前廳，接待室

例：The antechamber of the hall is already packed.
大廳的前廳早已擠滿了人。

❹ anticipate ▸ anti(before) + cip（拿取 = take）+ ate

v. 期望，預料

例：My professor anticipated that all of us write excellent papers.
我們的教授期待我們都寫出優異的報告。

❺ precaution ▸ pre + caution（注意）

n. 預防，警戒，預防措施

例：My brother brought a raincoat as a precaution on an overcast day.
天氣陰鬱，我弟弟帶了雨衣以防下雨。

❻ preliminary ▸ pre + limin（開端）+ ary

adj. 準備的，預備的，序言的 n. 準備，初步措施；初試

例：The Preliminary English Proficiency Test is easy. Don't worry.
初級英文程度測驗很簡單。不要擔心。

❼ preview ▸ pre + view（看）

v./n. 預覽

例：Can I get a preview of the book?
我可以先預覽這本書嗎？

❽ predetermine ▸ pre + determine（決定）

v. 先決，提前決定

例：My parents always predetermine everything for me.
我父母親總是預先替我決定好所有事。

❾ preschool ▸ pre + school

adj. 就學前的 n. 幼稚園

例：Public preschools are relatively cheaper than private ones.
公立幼稚園相對來說比私立的便宜。

Part2｜表示方向

post- 之後

❶ posterior ▸ post + erior

adj. 尾部的，後面的，隨後的

例：The posterior side of the building is abandoned.
這棟建物的後部已經廢棄了。

❷ posthumous

▸ post + hum（土壤 = earth）+ ous（被埋在地裡之後）

adj. 死後的，死後出版的

例：This collection is the late author's posthumous work.
這本選集是這位已故作家死後出版的作品。

❸ post meridiem ▸ post + meridiem(noon)

n. 下午（=in the afternoon），縮寫為p.m.

例：None of us attended the meeting held at 3 post meridiem.
我們沒有人參加下午三點舉行的會議。

❹ postmortem ▸ post + mort（死亡 = death）+ em

adj. 死後的，驗屍的 n. 驗屍，事後檢討

例：We'll have to carry out a postmortem brain test on your father's body.
我們必須要在你父親身體上作死後腦部檢測。

❺ postcensorship ▸ post + censorship

n. 事後檢查；事後審查

例：Postcencorship is meaningless since our products have already been launched.
事後審查沒有意義，因為我們的商品已經上市了。

❻ postgraduate ▸ post + graduate

adj. 大學畢業後的，研究生的 n. 研究生

例：My postgraduate life was filled with hard work and painstaking efforts.
我的研究生活充滿辛勤工作和費心努力。

❼ postnatal ▸ post + nat（出生）+ al

adj. 出生後的；產後的

例：Postnatal care is extremely important; I don't think you should save any penny.
產後護理非常重要，我不認為你需要省任何一筆錢。

❽ postscript ▸ post + script(writing)

n. （信件的）附言（縮寫為P.S.）

例：Read the postscript; it has the author's secret message.
讀附註，裡頭藏有作者的祕密訊息。

out- 向外；超過

❶ outcome ▶ out（向外）+ come

n. 結果

例：The outcome of the surgery was devastating.
手術結果令人痛心難受。

❷ outdoor ▶ out（向外）+ door（門）

adj. 室外的，戶外的

例：Outdoor activities are good for parent-children relationships.
戶外活動對親子關係是有益的。

❸ outlandish ▶ out（向外）+ land（土地）+ ish

adj. 奇異的，偏僻的，異國風格的

例：My twin cousins like to wear outlandish clothes and are not afraid of other's opinions.
我的雙胞胎堂弟喜歡穿奇裝異服，且不在意他人的評論。

❹ output ▶ out（向外）+ put（放置）

n. 產量，輸出

例：The output is decreasing and we all are afraid of getting fired.
輸出量減少，我們都害怕被裁員。

⑤ outgrow ▸ out（超過）+ grow

V. 長得穿不下（衣服），長得比……快

例：My niece has already outgrown her clothes. Time flies.
我的姪女已經長到穿不下她的衣服了。時光飛逝。

⑥ outlast ▸ out（超過）+ last（持續）

V. 比……持久，從……中逃生

例：This boxing competition is all about who can outlast another in the cage. 這場拳擊比賽就是在看誰能在籠子裡比對方撐得久。

⑦ outrun ▸ out（超過）+ run

V. 超過，比……跑得快

例：My brother said he can outrun me in the contest. He's bluffing.
我弟弟說他可以在比賽中跑贏我。他在吹牛。

⑧ outwit ▸ out（超過）+ wit（機智）

V.（智力上）超過，用聰明才智勝過

例：It's mind-blowing how a ten-year-old girl outwitted a professor in the competition.
看到一名十歲的女孩在比賽中以才智勝過一名教授，真是讓人驚訝。

⑨ outweigh ▸ out（超過）+ weigh

V. 重於，比……有價值，比……重要

例：The pros of the plan certainly outweigh the cons, if you are asking me. 若你詢問我的意見的話，此計畫的好處絕對是多過於壞處的。

ex- 向外；之前的

❶ explode ▸ ex + plod（大聲音） + e

v. 爆發，爆炸，激增

例：The bomb exploded all of a sudden. Fortunately, no one was hurt.
炸彈突然爆炸，所幸無人受傷。

❷ explore ▸ ex + plore（哭喊）

v. 探索，詳細調查，勘探

例：The world is out there for us to explore.
世界就在外頭，等著我們探索。

❸ exclaim ▸ ex + claim（叫喊）

v.（由於情緒激動）叫嚷

例：My mom exclaimed, “Don’t go there!”
我的媽媽大喊：「不要去那裡！」

❹ exit ▸ ex + it（走 = go）

n. 出口、通道

例：The exit is right over there. 出口就在那邊。

❺ export ▸ ex + port（運輸）

v./n. 輸出，出口

例：Our company doesn’t export masks anymore.
我們公司不再出口口罩了。

❻ extract ▶ ex + tract（拉）

v. 用力拉出、萃取、提煉 n. 萃取物

例：The serum is made with lily extracts.
這個精華液是用百合花萃取物製作的。

❼ expose ▶ ex + pose（放置）

v. 暴露

例：We should all avoid being exposed to second-hand smoking.
我們都應避免暴露在二手菸中。

❽ ex-husband

▶ ex（先前的）+ husband（丈夫）

n. 前夫

例：My ex-husband is a nice guy. We just don't get along anymore.
我的前夫是個好人，我們只是無法再相處下去。

❾ ex-soldier ▶ ex（先前的）+ soldier（軍人）

n. 退伍軍人

例：Both my grandfather and my father are ex-soldiers.
我的爺爺和父親都是退伍軍人。

Part2｜表示方向

over-、ultra- 超過

大致上，字首over-有兩種意思，一種同介詞over，表示「在……以上，超越」。另一種是過度「極其，極度」的意思。ultra帶有「beyond，exceedingly（過分地、超）」的意思。

❶ overcome ▸ over（超越）+ come

V. 克服，戰勝

例：You need to overcome your fear, or else you'll never get what you want.
你需要戰勝恐懼，不然你永遠得不到你想要的東西。

❷ overhear ▸ over（超越）+ hear

V. 偶然聽到，偷聽

例：I overheard my parent's conversation and learned that they were getting a divorce.
我偶然聽到父母的談話，並得知他們將要離婚。

❸ overtake ▸ over（超越）+ take

V. 趕上，超過，突然發生

例：The runner overtook the other one and landed first in the competition.
這名跑者超越了另外一位跑者，在比賽中得到第一。

❹ overthrow ▸ over（向上）+ throw

V. 推翻，打倒

例：People have full right to overthrow a corrupt government.
人們擁有完全的權利推翻貪腐的政府。

❺ overflow ▸ over（過度）+ flow（流）

v. 溢出，擠滿，充滿

例：The overflow of joy showed on her face.
她的臉上滿溢笑容。

❻ oversleep ▸ over（過度）+ sleep（睡）

v. 睡過頭，睡得太久

例：I overslept this morning and missed the bus.
我今天早上睡過頭，錯過了公車。

❼ overweight ▸ over + weight（重量）

adj. 超重的 v.（行李）超載（=overload）

例：Your luggage is overweight. You have to pay extra fees.
你的行李超重了，需付額外費用。

❽ ultrared ▸ ultra + red

adj. 紅外線的

例：This machine uses ultrared technique to detect viruses.
這台機器使用紅外線技術來偵測病毒。

❾ ultrasound ▸ ultra + sound

n. 超聲波

例：Many animals use ultrasound to communicate.
許多動物使用超聲波來溝通。

Part2｜表示方向

under-、sub-
下面；在……之下

字首意思和介詞under一樣，表示「在……下面，向下」的意思。另外還可以表示「比……不好的，比……低的」的意思。字首sub- 則可表示「under、below（在下面，向下）」的意思，主要有以下幾種拼寫變形。

❶ undergo ▸ under + go

v. 經歷，經受，忍受

例：I underwent a painful adolescence which leads to my distrust to the society. 我經歷過一段痛苦青春期，導致我對社會的不信任。

❷ undergraduate ▸ under + graduate（畢業生）

n. 大學生 adj. 大學生的

例：I'm still an undergraduate student, but I intend to apply for graduate schools.
我還是大學生，但我打算申請研究所。

❸ understand ▸ under + stand（在文章或話的下面站著）

v. 理解；明白

例：I don't understand you. Can you repeat it again?
我不懂你的意思。你可以再說一次嗎？

❹ undertake ▸ under + take（處理）

v. 承擔，從事

例：I am about to undertake two major projects next month.
我下個月將要承接兩項大型專案。

❺ undercharge ▸ under(inferior) + charge（較低的索價）

v. 少收……的款 n. 過低的索價（=an insufficient charge）

例：The customers were undercharged in that restaurant by almost 5% of the meal. 那間餐廳的客人被少收了將近用餐費的百分之五。

❻ underestimate ▸ under(inferior) + estimate（較低的評價）

v. 低估，輕視

例：The judges underestimated the contestant and were surprised by his performance. 評審們低估了這名選手，並對他的表現感到詫異。

❼ underprivileged ▸ under(inferior) + privileged（較低的權利）

adj.（在經濟或社會上）處於弱勢的，貧困的

例：If the government don't help the underprivileged, who will?
如果政府不幫助弱勢族群，誰會？

❽ submarine ▸ sub(under) + marine(sea)

adj. 海底的，海裡的 n. 潛水艇

例：The submarine missiles were said to be extremely powerful.
這些海底飛彈據説威力極度強大。

❾ subsidiary ▸ sub(under) + sid（坐= sit）+ i + ary

adj. 輔助的，補充的，附屬的，次要的 n. 輔助者，輔助物，子公司

例：The subsidiary of this corporation is located in Taiwan.
這間企業的子公司位在台灣。

❿ subdivide ▸ sub + divide（區分）

v. 再次細分

例：You need to subdivide the materials so you can better organize the procedure. 你需要再把材料細分，才能把流程架構地更好。

Part2｜表示方向

hyper-、epi- 在……之上；hypo- 在……之下

❶ hyperbole ▸ hyper + bole（丟 = throw）

adj.（修辭）誇張法

例：The hyperboles here and there truly enhance the dynamics of the book.

四處可見的誇飾法真的增加了這本書的活力。

❷ hypertension ▸ hyper + tens（伸 = strech） + ion

n. 高血壓，過度緊張

例：My grandfather has hypertension, so be careful not to make him angry.

我祖父有高血壓，所以要小心不要讓他生氣。

❸ hyperactive ▸ hyper + act + ive

n. 活動過度；過動症

例：My niece is a hyperactive child who has problem focusing.

我姪子是過動小孩，有專注力的問題。

❹ hypersensitive ▸ hyper + sens + itive

adj. 過於敏感的；過敏的

例：Being hypersensitive is good for creation sometimes.

有時候，高敏感對於創作是件好事。

❺ hyperlink ▸ hyper + link

n. 超連結

例：Click this hyperlink and it'll take you to the website you want to visit.
點一下這個超連結，它就會帶你去你想要瀏覽的網站。

❻ epidermal ▸ epi + derm（皮膚） + al

adj. 表皮的

例：Epidermal surgeries are usually done within an hour.
表皮手術通常都會在一個小時內結束。

❼ hypodermic ▸ hypo + derm（皮膚） + ic

adj. 皮下的

例：Hypodermic inflammation treatment often needs both medication and surgeries. 皮下發炎治療通常需要服藥和手術兩者。

❽ hypocrite ▸ hypo + crite

n. 偽善者

例：Don't be a hypocrite and only think about what you can get from the deal. 別當個偽善的人，只想著自己可以從交易中得到什麼好處。

❾ hypothesis ▸ hypo + thes（位置= to place） + is

n. 假設，前提

例：The hypothesis of your statement is that everyone can get an equal share of food. 你發言的前提是每個人都能得到均等的食物。

❿ hypotension ▸ hypo + tens（伸 = strech） + ion

n. 低血壓

例：Hypotension may sound less dangerous but it can also lead to death. 低血壓聽起來不危險，但它也能致死。

intra、intro、inter-、endo 在……之間

字首intra- 與 extra- 的意思相反，帶有「inside、inward」的意思。

❶ intraparty ▸ intra + party（黨）

adj. 黨內的，黨員間的

例：Intraparty disputes are unnecessary especially before the Presidential Election.
在總統大選前，黨內糾紛是不必要的。

❷ intrastate ▸ intra + state

adj. （美國州）內的

例：The government should really improve intrastate traffic systems.
政府真的應該改善州內交通系統。

❸ introspect ▸ intro + spect（看）

v. 內省（= look into one's own mind, feeling, etc.）

例：I am used to introspect before sleep.
我慣於在睡前自省。

❹ introvert ▸ intro + vert（轉 = turn）

n. 內向的人

例：I'm an introvert and don't like to attend social events.
我是個內向的人，不喜歡參加社交活動。

⑤ introduction ▶ intro + duct（引導 = lead）+ ion

n. 介紹

例：Should I make some introduction about the newly-released book?
我該替新發行的書做點介紹嗎？

⑥ intermingle ▶ inter + mingle（混合）

v. 混合在一起，（使）混合

例：Before you paint the wall, intermingle the colors first.
在漆牆之前，先將顏色混合在一起。

⑦ interpret ▶ inter + pret

v. 解釋；解讀，詮釋

例：Don't over-interpret the context, or you might misread the message from the work. 不要過度解讀文本，不然你可能會誤讀作品的訊息。

⑧ interweave ▶ inter + weave

v. 交織，交叉，混合

例：Human relationships are interweaved together.
人類之間的關係是交織在一起的。

⑨ endocrine ▶ endo + crine

n. 內分泌

例：Endocrine disorders may take a long time to treat.
內分泌失調可能會需要花長時間治療。

⑩ endoscope ▶ endo + scope（看；觀察儀器）

n. 內視鏡

例：Endoscopes are rarely used now.
內視鏡現在已經很少使用了。

Part2 | 表示方向

per-、dia-、trans- 穿越；徹底

❶ permanent ▶ per（完全地）+ man（留下）+ ent

adj. 永久的；永恆的

例：The scar may be permanent. Please be mentally prepared.
這個傷疤可能會是永久性的。請做好心理準備。

❷ perspective ▶ per + spect（看 = look）+ ive

n. 透視法；觀點 adj. 透視的

例：Your perspective on this issue is really ignorant.
你對此議題的觀點真的相當無知。

❸ perspire ▶ per + spire（呼吸 = breathe）

v. 流汗，分泌，滲出

例：The athlete perspired heavily after the marathon.
跑完馬拉松後，該名運動員汗如雨下。

❹ permit ▶ per + mit（傳送=send）v. 允許

例：Have your parents permitted you to go to the field trip?
你的父母親允許你參加校外教學了嗎？

❺ persist ▶ per + sist（站立 = stand）

v. 持續，堅持

例：If the rain persists, we might cancel the meeting.
如果雨持續下，我們可能會取消會議。

❻ diameter ▶ dia + meter

n. 直徑

例：Measure the diameter first before you continue the arithmetic.
先測量直徑，再繼續數學運算。

❼ diagonal ▶ dia + gon（角）+ al

adj. 對角線的，斜的

例：On the diagonal side of the room lies a 18-th century mahogany chair. 在房間對角線一處，放置著一張十八世紀的桃花心木椅。

❽ transient ▶ trans + ient

adj. 轉瞬即逝的，一時的，短暫的

例：The transient light made the night dreamy.
那轉瞬一逝的光讓夜晚如夢一般。

❾ transit ▶ trans + it (= go)

n. 通行，經過，輸送 v. 通過

例：Move pass through one next transit so the products can finish customs checking. 移動到下一個通道好讓商品可以結束海關檢測。

❿ transatlantic ▶ trans + atlantic（大西洋）

adj. 跨大西洋的

例：Transatlantic traveling is highly embraced now.
跨大西洋旅遊現在廣受歡迎。

Part3｜表示特質

mis- 錯誤的

❶ misbehavior ▸ mis(wrong) + behavior（行為）

n. 不當行為

例：Such misbehavior should be punished heavily.
如此不當行為應受重罰。

❷ mischief ▸ mis(wrong) + chief（首領）

n. 惡作劇，淘氣

例：Stop doing something out of mischief and get done to real business! 不要再調皮搗蛋了，趕快做正事！

❸ misfortune ▸ mis(wrong) + fortune（幸運）

n. 不幸，災難，不幸的事

例：Several events of misfortune occurred last night.
昨晚發生了幾起不幸事件。

❹ misgiving ▸ mis(wrong) + giving（給的東西）

n. 疑慮，不安，擔心

例：Don't harbor misgivings and find the solution as soon as you can.
別在心存疑慮，以最快的速度找出答案。

❺ mistake ▸ mis(wrong) + take（處理）

n. 錯誤，誤解 v. 弄錯，誤解

例：I made some minor mistakes in my paper and only got B + .
我在報告中犯了幾個小錯誤，只拿到B+。

⑥ mistrust ▶ mis(wrong) + trust（相信）

v./n. 不信任，懷疑，疑惑

例：Her mistrust toward me made me uneasy.
她對我的不信任讓我坐立不安。

⑦ misunderstand ▶ mis(wrong) + understand（理解）

v. 誤解

例：My sister misunderstood what I said and slapped me in the face.
我姊姊誤解我說的話，賞了我一巴掌。

⑧ misuse ▶ mis(wrong) + use（使用）

v./n. 誤用，虐待

例：The misuse of the machine may lead to unthinkable outcome.
誤用此機器可能會招致無可想像的後果。

⑨ mislead ▶ mis + lead（引導）

v. 錯誤引導

例：I was misled by the theory and hence reached a wrong conclusion.
我被此理論誤導，因此也得到了錯誤的結論。

⑩ mistreat ▶ mis + treat（對待）

v. 虐待

例：If you mistreat your pet, I'll call the police right away.
如果你虐待動物，我會馬上報警。

Part3 | 表示特質

in-、im-、il-、ir- 表否定

❶ illegible ▸ il + leg（讀） + ible

adj. 難以辨認的，難讀的

例：His handwriting is so illegible that I can't understand his teaching.
他的字跡太過潦草，以至於我無法理解他的教導。

❷ immature ▸ im + mature（成熟的）

adj. 不成熟的，未發育完全的

例：Stop acting like an immature child and be a man.
像個男子漢一點，別表現的像個不成熟的小孩。

❸ infirm ▸ in + firm（強健的 = strong）

adj. 弱的，意志薄弱的，虛弱的

例：Old and infirm, she lays on the bed all day. 她年邁體弱，整天躺在床上。

❹ irrelevant ▸ ir + relevant（相關的）

adj. 不相關的；不適切的；不對題的

例：What you just said is really irrelevant right now.
你剛剛說的話真的與現在的問題無關。

❺ impatient ▸ im + patient（有耐心的）

adj. 沒有耐心的，性急的

例：My mother is usually impatient and calls for efficiency.
我媽媽通常沒有耐性，要求效率。

⑥ inhuman ▸ in + human（人道的）

adj. 非人的；不人道的；沒有人性的

例：Such inhuman action should be sanctioned at once.
如此不人道的行為應受立即的制裁。

⑦ illegal ▸ il + legal（法律的）

adj. 違法的

例：Did you know that running through the red light is illegal?
你知道闖紅燈是違法的嗎？

⑧ irregular ▸ ir + reg（規則）+ ular

adj. 不規律的

例：The irregular beating of his heart causes him great pain.
心律不整造成他很大的痛苦。

⑨ illogical ▸ il + logic（邏輯）+ al

adj. 不合邏輯的

例：I can not tolerate your illogical thinking anymore. Let's divorce.
我無法再忍受你不合邏輯的思考方式了。離婚吧。

⑩ impure ▸ im + pure（純潔的）

adj. 不純潔的，不純的

例：Sex before marriage is considered impure by many Christians.
婚前性行為被許多基督教徒視為是不純潔的。

Part3｜表示特質

un- 表否定

❶ unable ▶ un + able（能……的）

adj. 不能的，沒有辦法的

例：I was unable to finish the paper before the deadline.
我無法在期限之前寫完報告。

❷ unaware ▶ un + aware（意識到的）

adj. 不知道的，沒意識到的

例：The politician is surely unaware of the potential backlash his statement may cause.
這名政客一定沒有意識到他的言論可能會引發強烈的反對。

❸ uncertain ▶ un + certain（確定的）

adj. 不確定的，猶豫的

例：I was still uncertain about whether to apply for a graduate school or not. 我仍然不確定是否要申請研究所。

❹ uncomfortable ▶ un + comfortable（舒服的）

adj. 令人不舒服的，不自在的（= uneasy）

例：Your remarks really made me uncomfortable, and I'm sure everyone felt the same.
你的言論讓我很不舒服，我相信其他人的感受也是如此。

❺ uncover ▶ un + cover（蓋子；掩護）

v. 揭發，暴露，揭開

例：The reporter uncovered the scandal of the two rising stars of the party. 這名記者揭發了該黨兩名明日之星的醜聞。

❻ undo ▸ un + do（做）

v. 取銷，解開（包裝或扣）

例：Can you help me undo the button of the dress on the back?
你能幫我解開裙子背後的扣子嗎？

❼ undress ▸ un + dress（穿）

v. 替……脫衣服，揭露

例：My mom undressed my little brother and gave him a quick shower.
我媽媽幫我弟弟褪去衣服，快速地替他洗了澡。

❽ unfold ▸ un + fold（折疊）

v. 展開，打開

例：Unfold the paper first before you apply the paints.
塗上顏料之前，先將紙攤開。

❾ unload ▸ un + load（裝載）

v. 卸貨，從……卸下

例：My father asked us to help unload the furniture on the truck.
我爸爸要我們幫忙把傢俱從貨車中卸下來。

❿ unlock ▸ un + lock（鎖）

v. 打開鎖，開啟

例：The locksmith unlocked the door for me at the cost of 1000 NTD.
鎖匠以一千元的價格替我開鎖。

Part3｜表示特質

anti-、counter-、contra- 反對、阻抗

❶ anti-aging ▸ anti + aging（老化）

adj. 抗老的

例：Do you want to try this anti-aging face cream?
你想試試看這款抗老臉霜嗎？

❷ antibody ▸ anti + body（身體）

n. 抗體

例：We need to know what kind of antibody it is before we know how to combat the disease. 我們需要知道這是何種抗體，才能得知如何抗疫。

❸ antivirus ▸ anti + virus（病毒）

adj. 防毒的

例：This antivirus software can protect your computer on all aspects.
這個防毒軟體可以在所有層面上防護你的電腦。

❹ antiwar ▸ anti + war（戰爭）

adj. 抗戰的

例：Anti-war campaigns are on full fledge now.
抗戰運動如火如荼地展開。

❺ counterpart ▸ counter + part（部分）

n. 相似物或人，與自己擁有相似職責或處在相似位置的人

例：In terms of style, these two pair of jeans are exact counterparts.
就風格上來說，這兩款牛仔褲幾乎一樣。

❻ contrary ▶ contr(a) + ary

adj. 相反的，完全不同的 n. 相反（的事物） adv. 相反地

例：On the contrary, I hope you all the best. I don't hold grudges.
相反地，我毫無怨恨，祝你幸福。

❼ contrast ▶ contra + st

v. 對比，對照 n. 顯著差異，對照

例：The stark contrast between these two writers' theories is rather intriguing. 這兩位作家的理論之間的強烈對比相當有趣。

❽ counterattack ▶ counter + attack（攻擊）

n. 逆襲，反擊

例：The country launched a counterattack and won the war.
這個國家發起反擊，贏了戰爭。

❾ contradict ▶ contra + dict（說 = say）

v. 牴觸；矛盾；駁斥

例：Are you aware that your words contradict your actions?
你有意識到你言行不一嗎？

❿ counterclockwise

▶ counter + clockwise（順時針的）

adj./adv. 逆時針方向的（地）

例：The water flowed counterclockwise and formed an optical illusion.
水往逆時鐘方向流動，形成一種視覺錯視。

Part3｜表示特質

dis- 否定；分離

❶ disagree ▶ dis(not) + agree（同意）

v. 意見不一致，意見不同，吵架，爭吵，不適宜

例：I think we can agree to disagree here.
我想在這裡我們可以尊重彼此不同的意見。

❷ disappear ▶ dis(not) + appear（出現）

v. 不見，消失，滅絕

例：The magician suddenly disappeared on the stage.
魔術師突然在舞台上消失不見了。

❸ disintegrate ▶ dis(not) + integrate（合併）

v. 使某物碎裂，使崩潰，崩潰

例：The vase disintegrated due to the earthquake.
因為地震，花瓶碎了一地。

❹ disable ▶ dis(not) + able（能夠）

v. 使失去能力，殘疾，使無資格

例：I was disabled after the car crash. 在車禍意外後我成為了殘疾人士。

❺ dishonest ▶ dis(not) + honest（正直的，誠實的）

adj. 不正直的，不誠實的

例：Being dishonest and selfish will eventually make you a heartless man. 不誠實和自私最終會使你成為一個無情的人。

❻ disregard ▸ dis(not) + regard（注意）

V. 無視；無視，不關心

例：His constant disregard of his health led him to demise.
他對健康的長期忽視導致其死亡。

❼ distract ▸ dis(not) + tract

V. 使分心

例：The film temporarily distracted me from all the nuisance.
這部電影短暫地使我不去想所有煩心的事。

❽ disperse ▸ dis(away) + (s)pers（散落） + e

V. 驅離、分散

例：The police dispersed the protests in a peaceful way.
警方用和平的方式驅離的抗議人士。

❾ distribute ▸ dis(away) + tribute（分配）

V. 分配，分發，散佈

例：The manager asked the staff to distribute the leaflets on the street.
經理要求職員到街上發傳單。

Part3 | 表示特質

ab-、se- 分離；離開

❶ abnormal ▶ ab + normal（正常的）

adj. 不正常的

例：The boy's abnormal behavior caught everyone's attention.
這個小男孩異常的舉動引起了所有人的注意。

❷ abduct ▶ab + duct（引導）

v. 綁架

例：The villain abducted the little girl and arouse anger from the public.
壞人綁走了小女孩，引發公憤。

❸ abnegate ▶ab + neg（否定的）+ ate

v. 放棄（權力等），克制（慾望等）

例：The governor abnegated his power and retired at once.
統領者放棄權力，即刻退休。

❹ absent ▶ ab + sent（存在）

adj. 不在場的，缺席的

例：I expect no one to be absent on the final exam.
我期望在期末考時沒有人缺席。

❺ abrupt ▶ ab + rupt（爆裂）

adj. 突然的，陡峭的

例：The abrupt heavy blowing of the wind scared me.
突然的一陣強風嚇到了我。

⑥ secede ▶ se + cede（走）

v. 脫離，退出，分離

例：I bet many countries want to secede from this so-called international organization now.
我猜現在應該有很多國家想要退出這個所謂的國際組織。

⑦ separate ▶ se + parate（準備）

v. 分離，分開，分居 adj. 分離的，個別的，單獨的

例：We lived in separate rooms to avoid gossips.
為了避免八卦，我們住在不同的房間。

⑧ sever ▶ se + ver

v. 切斷，中斷，使分離

例：The examiner severed the head from the body for further autopsy.
檢查人員將頭部從身體切斷以便進一步驗屍。

⑨ segregate ▶ se + greg（群體） + ate

v. 隔離

例：Segregate people based on race and gender is absurd.
以種族和性別隔離人民是荒謬的。

⑩ seduce ▶ se + duce（引導）

v. 引誘

例：No one can seduce me with any kind of food when I'm on a diet!
在我節食期間沒有人能以任何一種食物誘惑我！

Part3｜表示特質

bene-、bon-、eu- 好的

❶ benefit ▶ bene + fit（製作 = make）

n. 好處，利益（=profit） v. 助於

例：This medicine is going to benefit you in the long term.
這個藥長期來說對你會有好處。

❷ benevolent ▶ bene + vol（意志 = will） + ent

adj. 仁慈的，好意的，慈善的

例：The man has a benevolent heart toward everyone.
男子對所有人都抱持著一顆良善的心。

❸ benign ▶來自拉丁字源，表示「招致」了「好的事物」

adj. 善良的，好意的，良性的

例：This is a benign tumor. Take some rest first.
這是良性腫瘤。先好好休息。

❹ benediction ▶ bene + dict（說 = say） + ion

n. 讚美、祝福

例：With my loved one's benediction, I went on a long journey in Europe. 帶著我所愛之人的祝福，我啟程往歐洲進行長途旅行。

❺ bona fide ▶ bona + fide（信仰 = faith）

adj. 真實的

例：Make sure it is a bona fide company before you invest in it.
在投資之前，先確認這間公司是不是影子公司。

❼ bonus ▶ bon + us

n. 特別紅利，獎金

例：My brother received a high number of year-end bonus.
我哥哥領到了很高數目的年終獎金。

❽ eulogy ▶ eu + logy（言說= speech）

n. 頌詞，讚頌

例：This eulogy was made for singing at the first place.
這首頌詞一開始就是為了歌唱進行製作的。

❾ euphony ▶ eu + phony（聲音 = sound）

n. 悅耳的聲音，音調和諧

例：Where does such euphony come from?
這優美的聲音從何而來？

❿ euthanasia ▶ eu + thanas（死亡 = death） + ia

n. 安然去世，安樂死

例：He went to Switzerland for euthanasia and we all gave him our benediction.
他前往瑞士進行安樂死，我們都給予了祝福。

Part3｜表示特質

mal- 惡的

❶ malevolence ▶ mal + e + vol（意志 = will）+ ence

n. 惡意，壞心

例：Having a heart of malevolence will make you resentful everyday.
擁有一顆壞心，你每天都會充滿怨懟。

❷ malady ▶ mal + ady（受制；習慣 = hold）

n. 疾病，弊病

例：The incurable malady was the reason of such high mortality rate back in the 14th century.
此不治之病是十四世紀死亡率如此高的原因。

❸ malice ▶ mal + ice（表行為或狀態）

n. 惡意，怨恨，敵意

例：The revenge was made from malice and hostility.
這場報復純粹出於惡意與敵意。

❹ malefactor ▶ mal + e + fact（做）+ or

n. 作惡者；或壞事的人

例：I hope the malefactor can be sentence to jail forever.
我希望此滋生事端的人可以被終生監禁。

❺ malnutrition ▶ mal + nutrition（營養）

n. 營養失調

例：Over half of the global population suffer from malnutrition.
有超過全球一半以上的人口營養失調。

⑥ maladjustment ▶ mal + adjustment（調整）

n. 失調，不適應

例：Mental maladjustment is expected if anticipated living standards are not met with.
若沒有達到預期的生活標準，心理失調是可期的。

⑦ malfunction ▶ mal + function（功能）

n. 故障

例：Improper care of the equipment led to its malfunctions from time to time.
維護不周導致這個設備時不時會故障。

⑧ malformation ▶ mal + form（形狀） + ation

n. 畸形

例：The malformation of the product is the result of inaccurate arithmetic.
因為有失精準的運算，此產品形狀有異。

⑨ malpractice ▶ mal + practice（準則）

n. 弊端；不當行為，治療不當，誤診

例：The doctor was faced with a lawsuit due to constant malpractice.
這名醫生因為不當醫療行為面臨法律糾紛。

Part3｜表示特質

con-、com-、co- 一起的

❶ consolidate ▸ con + solid（整體）+ ate

v. 合併（學校或公司等），鞏固

例：These two firms are going to consolidate and form a bigger one.
這兩間公司會合併成一間更大的。

❷ converge ▸ con + verge（彎曲 = bend）

v. 集合，集中，會合

例：The two minor rivers converge here and flow into the sea.
這兩條支流在此匯合流向大海。

❸ cooperate ▸ co + oper（運作）+ ate

v. 合作，配合

例：We should cooperate and complete this project by the end of next week. 我們應該合作，於下週末前完成此專案。

❹ commensurate ▸ com + mens（測量）+ ate

adj. 大小相同的，範圍或程度一致的，相當的（符合的）

例：A government's authority should be commensurate with its responsibility. 一個政府應權責相當。

❺ compatible ▸ com + pati（感受）+ ble

adj. 相容的，能共處的

例：This wire is not compatible with the machine. 這個電線和機器不合。

❻ comrade ▶ 源自chamber，有「房間」的意思

n. 同事，朋友，黨員

例：Comrades! Let's fight for our country!
夥伴們！一起為我們的國家而戰！

❼ condensation ▶ con + dens（濃的） + ation

n. 凝縮，壓縮

例：You need to wait for full condensation of the liquid before doing anything else.
在進行其他事之前，你必須先等待液體完全凝固。

❽ conclude ▶ con + clude（關閉）

v. 做結論、以……做結束

例：The student concluded the presentation with a well-made graph.
學生以製作良好的表格結束報告。

❾ compete ▶ com + pete（奮鬥；尋找）

v. 競爭

例：These companies no longer compete with one another, but cooperate to help the citizen.
這幾間公司不再相互競爭，而是合作幫助人民。

❿ compassion ▶ com + pass（情感） + ion

n. 同情（心）

例：The lack of compassion may make you a selfish person.
缺乏同情心可能會使你成為一個自私的人。

Part3｜表示特質

syn-、sym- 一起；同時

❶ synchronize ▸ syn + chron(time) + ize

v. （使）同時發生，使同步

例：You have to synchronize these two procedures, or else the result may be inaccurate.
你必須同步這兩個步驟，不然你的結果可能會不準確。

❷ syndrome ▸ syn + drome（跑）

n. 症候群

例：Down syndrome is relatively uncommon due to pre-natal tests now.
因為產前檢測，唐氏症現在相對來説已經很少見了。

❸ symbiosis ▸ sym + bio（生命） + sis

n. 共生

例：Human society is also a form of symbiosis, isn't it?
人類社會也是共生一種，不是嗎？

❹ symmetry ▸ sym + metr（測量） + y

n. 左右對稱，對稱，均衡

例：This piece of painting was done with a perfect symmetry of a hand-drawn butterfly's wings.
這幅畫是以一隻手繪蝴蝶之翅的完美對稱所完成的。

❺ symptom ▶ sym + ptom（降臨）

n. 徵兆，前兆，症狀

例：The symptoms of this disease is constant coughing and slight fever.
這個疾病的症狀是不斷地咳嗽和輕微發燒。

❻ synopsis ▶ syn + op（看） + sis

n. 梗概，大綱

例：The synopsis of this piece of writing is the existential meaning of human beings.
這篇作品的大綱是人類的存在意義。

❼ synonym ▶ syn + onym（名字）

n. 同義詞

例：Beautiful and pretty are sometimes considered synonyms.
「漂亮的」和「美麗的」有時被視為是同義詞。

❽ synthesis ▶ syn + the（放置） + sis

n. 綜合，合成

例：In this experiment, the synthesis of A and B will become E.
在這個實驗裡，A 和 B 的合成會成為 E。

❾ sympathy ▶ sym + path（情感） + y

n. 同情

例：Should you have sympathy toward others, you wouldn't be treated this way. 如果你對他人保有同情，你就不會遭受這般待遇。

Part3｜表示特質

re- 回返；再次

字首re-一般用作「back（向後），again（再，再次）」的意思。主要有以下幾種形態變化。

❶ rebuke ▶ re(back) + buke（打=beat）

v./n. 指責；訓斥

例：My parents rebuked me for playing with fire in thekitchen.
我爸媽訓斥我在廚房玩火。

❷ recommend ▶ re(back) + commend（稱讚）

v. 推薦

例：Can you recommend some books on English literature?
你可以推薦我一些英國文學的書嗎？

❸ research ▶ re(again) + search（尋找）

n./v. 研究，調查，探究

例：Do some research before you turn in your paper.
在繳交報告之前，做點功課。

❹ retrieve ▶ re(again) + trieve（尋找 = find）

v. 回收，取回

例：Can you retrieve the box under the table for me?
你可以幫我從桌子底下取出箱子嗎？

❺ refund ▶ re(back) + fund（傾注）

v. 退款

例：They refused to refund me! I'm going to file for a lawsuit!
他們拒絕退款！我要告他們！

❻ repair ▸ re(again) + pair

V. 修補；修理

例：My father repaired his car on his own.
我爸爸自己修理車子。

❼ renew ▸ re(agin) + new（新的）

V. 更新

例：Remember to renew the membership by the end of this week.
記得在週末之前續約會員資格。

❽ redo ▸ re(again) + do（做）

V. 重新做

例：My professor asked me to redo the paper because I didn't do enough research.
我的教授要求我重做報告，因為我沒有做足夠的研究。

❾ recall ▸ re(again) + call（呼叫）

V. 回想

例：Sitting under the tree, I recalled some beautiful memories.
坐在樹下，我回想起一些美麗的時光。

❿ retract ▸ re(back) + tract（拉）

V. 收回、撤回

例：The official retracted his statement under the pressure of public opinions. 在大眾輿論的壓力之下，該官員撤回言論。

Part3｜表示特質

super-、sur- 超過

❶ superb ▸ super + b

adj. 極好的，優秀的，傑出的，壯麗的

例：You've done a superb job! 你做得真好！

❷ superior ▸ super + ior

adj. 品質較好的，上級的，位置較高的

例：This bunch of wood is of superior quality.
這批木頭的品質較好。

❸ surround ▸ sur + round（使圓形）

v. 包圍，圍繞

例：I was surround by my loved ones everyday and I feel blessed.
我每天都被我愛之人圍繞且覺得幸福。

❹ superficial ▸ super + fic（做） + ial（形容詞字尾）

adj. 表面的、膚淺的

例：If you judge a book by its cover, you're a superficial person.
如果你以貌取人，那麼你就是個膚淺的人。

❺ surface ▸ sur + face（表面）

n. 表面

例：On the surface, the table looks sturdy.
就表面上來看，這個桌子看起來很穩固。

⑥ surveillance ▶ sur + veil（看） + ance

n. 監視，守望，指揮，監督

例：Under surveillance, the prisoners behaved well.
在監視之下，犯人表現良好。

⑦ surpass ▶ sur + pass（走）

v. 超越、勝過……

例：The speaker delivered an amazing speech that surpassed all others.
這位講者完成了一場精彩的演講，勝過他人。

⑧ surreal ▶ sur + real（真實的）

adj. 超現實的

例：The surreal elements of this film add up the whole mystic atmosphere.
這部電影的超現實元素增加了整體的謎樣氛圍。

⑨ supersonic ▶ super + son（聲音） + ic

adj. 超音波的

例：This particular supersonic equipment is rather dangerous.
特別是這台超聲波設備，相當危險。

⑩ surname ▶ sur + name（名字）

n. 別名，姓

例：Fill in the blank with your surname.
將空白處填上你的姓。

Part3｜表示特質

pseudo- 假的

❶ pseudonym ▸ pseud(o) + nym（名字）

n. 匿名，假名，筆名

例：Why did he write the book under a pseudonym?
他為什麼要匿名寫這本書？

❷ pseudoscience ▸ pseudo + science（科學）

n. 偽科學

例：This is not pseudoscience. It has solid proof.
這不是偽科學，其擁有紮實的證據。

❸ pseudograph ▸ pseudo + graph（寫 = write）

n. 偽書，偽圖

例：This is taken as a pseudograph, so no proper studies have been done so far.
這被視為是偽書，所以目前並沒有人認真研究它。

❹ pseudo-democratic ▸ pseudo + demo（人民） + cratic

adj. 假民主的

例：We're all living in this pseudo-democratic society and when can we be saved from such illusion?
我們都活在這假民主的社會之中，何時我們才能從如此幻象中解脫？

Part3 | 表示特質

quasi- 假的；一半的

❶ quasi-military ▸ quasi + milit（軍事） + ary

adj. 半軍事的

例：This quasi-military organization has been conducting corrupt deals for decades.

這個半軍事組織幾十年來進行腐敗勾當。

❷ quasi-legal ▸ quasi + legal（法律的）

adj. 半法定的

例：Don't agree to quasi-legal negotiation before you know your own right.

在知悉自身權益之前，別同意半法定的協商。

❸ quasi-scientific ▸ quasi + sci（知道） + en + tific

adj. 偽科學的

例：This piece of quasi-scientific information wouldn't receive academic approval.

這項偽科學資訊不會得到學術認可。

❹ quasi-government

▸ quasi + govern（治理） + ment

adj. 半國營的

例：The quasi-government unit has done a lot to assist the under-privileged.

這個半國營單位做了很多事幫助弱勢族群。

Part3｜表示特質

hetero- 不同的；homo- 相同的

❶ heterogeneous ▸ hetero + gen（出生）+ eous

adj. 由很多種類組成的

例：A heterogeneous community is where I want to live.
我想住在由不同種族人口組成的社區。

❷ heterogenesis ▸ hetero + gen（出生）+ esis

n. 異殖；（生物）突變

例：Heterogensis to some extent contribute to the diversity of all living beings.
異性生殖某程度上對生物多樣性做出了貢獻。

❸ heterosexual ▸ hetero + sexual（性的）

adj. 異性戀的 n. 異性戀者

例：Most animals are heterosexual, and it's only one form of sexual orientations.
大部分的動物皆是異性相吸，且僅是性傾向的其中一種。

❹ heterodox ▸ hetero + dox（信仰）

adj. 異端的；非正統的

例：Such heterodox statement has met with harsh criticism.
如此非正統言論已遭受嚴厲批判。

❺ homeopathy ▸ homeo + pathy（感受= feeling）

n. 順勢療法

例：To be frank, homeopathy is pseudo-scientific and I don't agree to it.
老實說，順勢療法是偽科學，我不贊同。

❻ homocentric ▸ homo + centr（中心）+ ic

adj. 具有同一中心的，同心的，共心的

例：Look closely, and you will discover that these circles are actually homocentric.
仔細看，你就會發現這些圓是同心的。

❼ homonym ▸ homo + nym（名字）

n. 同音異義詞，同名之人，同名之物

例："Book" is a homonym with two meanings: something to read and to make a reservation.
「書」是同音異義字，有兩個意思：閱讀之物與預約。

❽ homosexual ▸ homo + sexual（性的）

adj. 同性戀的 n. 同性戀者

例：Being a homosexual isn't up to one's choice.
同性戀並非個人自身能選擇的。

Chapter 2
字根 *Root*

Part1｜人體&社會

anim 生命、精神

❶ animal ▶ anim(life) + al

n. 動物 adj. 動物的，動物性的，野獸一般的

例：I am an animal lover and I go to the zoo frequently.
我喜歡動物，並常常去動物園。

❷ animate ▶ anim(life) + ate（動詞字尾）

v. 賦予……以生命，使有生氣 adj. 有生命的，有生氣的

例：The brush strokes at the end suddenly animated the whole painting. 最後的筆觸瞬間賦予了這幅畫整體的生命力。

❸ inanimate ▶ in(not) + anim(life) + ate

adj. 沒有生命力的，沒有活力的

例：Inanimate objects exert their influence on us in an invisible way.
靜物以無法看見的方式影響著我們。

❹ magnanimity ▶ magn（大的） + anim + ity

n. 寬宏大量，雅量

例：The old man show his magnanimity and forgave the rude little boy.
老人展現了寬宏大量，原諒了無理的小男孩。

❺ unanimity ▶ un(i)（一） + animity

n. 全體一致，一致同意

例：I hope we can reach unanimity during this year-end meeting.
我希望在此場年終會議我們可以達成意見一致。

anthrop 人

❶ anthropology ▶ anthrop + ology（研究）

n. 人類學

例：The study of anthropology entails great efforts and patience.
修習人類學需要很多努力和耐心。

❷ philanthropy ▶ phil（愛 = love）+ anthrop + y

n. 博愛，慈善，慈善事業

例：Donations are acts of philanthropy and we should all chip in.
捐贈是慈善行為的一種，我們都應出一點錢。

❸ misanthropy ▶ mis（表否定）+ anthropy

n. 厭世

例：His words exhibit a slight sense of misanthropy and some may not like it. 他的文字展現出些微的厭世感，有些人可能會不喜歡。

❹ anthropomorphism ▶ anthrop + o + morph（行為 = form）+ ism

n. 擬人論，擬人觀，擬人化

例：Anthropomorphism is a kind of literary techniques.
擬人是一種文學技巧。

❺ misanthrope ▶ mis（表否定）+ anthrop + e

n. 厭世者；不願與人來往者

例：Billy is such a misanthrope that everyone can sense his negative energy. 比利真是個厭世的人，每個人都可以感受到他的負能量。

bio 生命、生物

❶ biologist ▸ bio + logist（表示人的字尾）

n. 生物學家

例：Both of my grandparents are biologists and I wish to become one in the future. 我們祖父母都是生物學家，我希望我未來也是。

❷ biography ▸ bio + graphy（紀錄）

n. 傳記，傳記文學

例：The biography of John Lennon is really worth a read.
約翰藍儂的傳記非常值得一看。

❸ autobiography ▸ auto(self) + bio + graphy（紀錄）

n. 自傳

例：I encourage my mother, a prestigious researcher, to write an autobiography. 我鼓勵我母親——一名具有聲望的研究員——寫自傳。

❹ biochemistry ▸ bio + chemistry（化學）

n. 生物化學

例：Biochemistry is really difficult for me. It's like rocket science.
生物化學對我來說非常難，簡直無法理解。

❺ biosphere ▸ bio + sphere（球）

n. 生物圈

例：All living beings dwell in biospheres that constitute the earth.
所有的生物都住在生物圈，其構成地球。

card, cor, cord, cour 心

❶ cordial ▸ cord + ial

adj. 發自真心的，誠心誠意的

例：We are greeted with a cordial welcome from the host.
我們受到主人誠心歡迎。

❷ courage ▸ cour + age（名詞字尾）

n. 勇氣，膽量

例：I couldn't pluck up the courage to say goodbye.
我無法鼓起勇氣道別。

❸ cardiac ▸ card + iac（表某性質的）

adj. 心臟（病）的 n. 強心劑，心臟病患者

例：Cardiac arrest may cause death all of a sudden.
心搏停止可能會導致瞬間死亡。

❹ cardinal ▸ cardin + al

adj. 重要的，基本的 n. 紅衣主教，深紅色

例：These four rocks represent the cardinal points of the architecture.
這四個石頭代表著這個建築的四個基本基點。

❺ concord ▸ con（一起的）+ cord

n. 一致，和諧

例：I hope all countries can live in concord hereafter.
我希望以後所有國家都能和諧共處。

Part1 | 人體&社會

civi 公民

❶ civic ▸ civ(citizen) + ic

adj. 城市的，市民的

例：The civic center is where most of the demonstrations take place.
大多遊行都在市中心舉行。

❷ civil ▸ civ(city) + il

adj. 民間的，市民的，民事的，文明的

例：This case is ruled as a civil one, so you might have to go to the other department.
這個案件裁定為民事案件，所以你可能要去另一個部門。

❸ civilian ▸ civil(city) + ian（表示人的字尾）

n. 平民 adj. 平民的

例：The party eventually won and established a civilian government.
該黨最終獲勝，建立了平民政府。

❹ civilize ▸ civil(city) + ize（動詞字尾）

v. 使文明（化）

例：A highly-civilized society is the government's ultimate goal.
一個高度文明化的社會是政府的終極目標。

❺ civilization ▸ civ + il + iz(e) + ation

n. 文明

例：Western civilizationis much differentiate from Eastern ones.
西方文明和東方文明有許多差異。

Part1 | 人體&社會

corp 身體

❶ corpse ▸ 從「身體」上產生出來

n. 屍體

例：Look at the corpse. He must undergo huge pain before he died.
看看這具屍體。他在死前肯定遭受相當大的痛苦。

❷ corporal ▸ corpor(body) + al

adj. 肉體的，身體的 n. 下士

例：We all are corporal beings and the desire to live forever should be abandoned. 我們都是肉身存在，應該捨棄想長生不了的念頭。

❸ corpulent ▸ corp + ulent（充滿的）

adj. 肥胖的

例：Since when did he become so corpulent?
他什麼時候變得這麼胖的？

❹ corporation ▸ corpor(body) + ation（名詞字尾）

n. 團體，公司，法人

例：This corporation should be eliminated at once.
這個腐敗的組織應該被立即消除。

❺ incorporate ▸ in(into) + corpor + ate

v. 合併

例：The designer incorporated the element of Chinese calligraphy into the book cover. 設計師將中國書法元素加入至書封。

Part1 | 人體&社會

derm 皮膚

❶ dermatology ▶ dermat(skin) + ology（研究 = study）

n. 皮膚醫學，皮膚科學

例：Dermatology is in trend now since everyone wants to get their face lifted. 皮膚科學現在正當紅，因為每個人都想去拉皮。

❷ epidermis ▶ epi（之上 = upon）+ dermis

n. 表皮，外皮

例：The epidermis of alligators are hard as rocks.
鱷魚的表皮硬得像石頭。

❸ hypodermic ▶ hypo（之下 = under）+ derm(skin) + ic

adj. 皮下的 n. 皮下注射，皮下注射器

例：Hypodermic needles should be sterilized before used.
皮下注射針在使用之前應進行消毒。

❹ dermatitis ▶ dermat(skin) + itis

n. 皮炎

例：My grandmother has been suffering from an incurable dermatitis.
我的祖母飽受無法治癒的皮炎之苦。

❺ dermotologist ▶ dermat(skin) + ologist（表示人的字尾）

n. 皮膚科醫生

例：That dermatologist is really professional; everyone speak highly of her. 那位皮膚科醫生非常專業，每個人都對她讚譽有加。

demo 人民

❶ democracy ▸ demo + cracy（統治）

n. 民主政治，民主政體

例：I hope all people around the world can live in democracy.
我希望全世界的人都能活在民主之中。

❷ demography ▸ demo + graphy（書寫，紀錄）

n. 人口統計學

例：According to the demography, elderly people is reaching record high. 根據人口統計，老年人口正創新高。

❸ endemic ▸ en(in) + dem(peole) + ic

adj. 地方性疾病的，某地特有的

例：This disease is no longer endemic. It's pandemic now.
這個疾病已經不局限於地方傳染，開始廣為流行了。

❹ democratic ▸ demo + crat（統治）+ ic

adj. 民主的

例：Who doesn't want to live in a democratic society?
誰不想要住在民主社會？

❺ epidemic ▸ epi(upon) + dem + ic

adj. 流行性的，傳染性的，極為盛行的 n. 流行病

例：It look the government a lot of efforts to control this epidemic.
政府花費了相當大的力氣控制此流行病。

ego 自我

❶ egoist ▸ ego(self) + is（表示人的字尾）

n. 利己主義者（= a believer in egoism）

例：He is such an egoist that no one wants to be friends with him
他真是個利己主義者，沒有人想要和他當朋友。

❷ egocentric ▸ ego(self) + centr + ic

adj. 以自我為中心的 n. 自我中心主義者

例：If you continue to be this egocentric, you'll fail eventually.
如果你一直以自我為中心，你最終會失敗。

❸ superego ▸ super(over) + ego(self)

n. 超我

例：Superego represents the ideal state one wants to reach.
超我代表著一個人想要追求的理想境界。

❹ alter ego ▸ alter(other) + ego(self)

n. 第二自我，好朋友

例：I'm an engineer, but editor is my alter ego.
我是名工程師，但另一部分的我是一名編輯。

❺ egoistical ▸ ego + ist + ical

adj. 自私自利的，利己主義的

例：He's not only pretentious, but also egotistical and mean.
他不僅自視甚高，還自私且尖酸刻薄。

Part1 | 人體&社會

hypno、narco、somn 睡眠

❶ hypnotize ▶ hypnot + ize（動詞字尾）

v. 對……催眠，使著迷

例：In the film, she tried to hypnotize her daughter's boyfriend just to kidnap him. 在這部電影中，她試圖催眠她女兒的男朋友以便綁架他。

❷ hypnotic ▶ hypno + tic

adj. 催眠的，有催眠作用的 n. 安眠藥

例：Hypnotics are prescribed medication. 安眠藥是處方藥。

❸ narcotic ▶ narco + tic

adj. 麻醉的，毒品的 n. 麻醉劑，毒品

例：We will inject some narcotic drug into your body before the operation. 在手術之前，我們會替你注射麻醉藥。

❹ insomnia ▶ in(not) + somn + ia

n. 失眠

例：I've been suffering from insomnia for months.
我受失眠之苦好幾個月了。

❺ somnambulism ▶ somn + ambul（走 = walk）+ ism

n. 夢遊

例：Fortunately, there's cure for somnambulism now.
幸運的是，現在已經有藥可以治療夢遊了。

gen 生產

❶ gender ▶ gen + der

n. 性別

例：Gender equality is oftentimes misunderstood and has a long way to go. 性別平等常為人誤解，還有很長的路要走。

❷ genetic ▶ gene(birth) + tic（研究）

adj. 遺傳的，基因的

例：This disease is genetic, so you better do annual health checkup. 這種疾病是遺傳性的，所以你最好每年去做健康檢查。

❸ genealogy ▶ gene(birth) + a + logy（研究，學說）

n. 系譜學，家譜

例：You can look up your genealogy if you want to know more about your history. 想更瞭解你的歷史，你可以查看你的族譜。

❹ generate ▶ gener(birth) + ate(make)

v. 使發生，形成

例：This machine generates a special kind of element that help preserve water. 這台機器會生成一種特殊的物質幫助水的儲存。

❺ genius ▶ geni + us

n. 天才，天資

例：Ms. Tang is such a genius. Her invention helps all the citizens. 唐小姐真是天才，她的發明幫助了所有的市民。

cogn、gno、sci 知道

❶ diagnosis ▸ dia(through) + gno + sis

n. 診斷

例：According to the diagnosis, this is a benign tumor.
根據診斷，這是良性腫瘤。

❷ recognize ▸ re(again) + cogn + ize

v. 認出，賞識

例：Sorry. I didn't recognize you just now. 抱歉。我剛剛沒認出你來。

❸ incognito ▸ in(not) + cogn + ito

adj. 隱姓埋名的

例：If you want to remain incognito, keep a low profile.
若你想要隱姓埋名，就得行事低調。

❹ science ▸ sci + ence（名詞字尾）

n. 科學

例：My brother chose political science as his major.
我弟弟選政治學當作主修。

❺ conscious ▸ con + sci + ous（形容詞字尾）

adj. 有意識的，意識到的

例：I'm fully conscious of the consequence I'm going to face.
我非常清楚我將要面對的後果。

lingu 語言、舌頭；liter 文字

❶ lingual ▸ lingu(tongue) + al

adj. 語言的，舌的，舌音的 **n.** 舌音（字）

例：Lingual nerves is what makes us sense whatever excites our tongue. 舌神經是讓我們知覺到刺激我們舌頭事物的要件。

❷ bilingual ▸ bi(two) + lingu + al

adj. 雙語的

例：My parents taught us both Japanese and English when we were little. So both my sister and I are bilingual.
我的父母從小教導我們日文和英文。所以我姊姊和我都會説兩種語言。

❸ literal ▸ liter + al

adj. 字面的，逐字的

例：Literal translation is the most common form of translations.
逐字翻譯是最常見的翻譯方式。

❹ literary ▸ liter + ary

adj. 文學的

例：Believe it or not. This literary work was written by me.
信不信由你。這部文學作品是我寫的。

❺ obliterate ▸ ob(against) + liter + ate

v. 消滅，消除，忘掉

例：I wish I could obliterate all my painful memories.
我希望我可以消除所有痛苦的回憶。

milit 軍事

❶ militant ▶ milit + ant

adj. 好戰的，激進的，交戰的 n. 好戰者，激進份子

例：The protesters grew more and more militant and the issue lost focus. 抗議份子變得越來越激進，議題已失焦。

❷ militarize ▶ militar(y) + ize（動詞字尾）

v. 軍事化

例：It seemed that the president was trying to militarize the whole educational system. 這名校長看來是想要將整個教育體系軍事化。

❸ military ▶ milit + ary

adj. 軍人的，軍事的 n. 軍人；軍隊

例：My brother finally made a decision and registered for the military. 我弟弟終於下定決心服役。

❹ militia ▶ milit + ia →軍隊化的事物

n. 義勇軍，民兵組織，民兵，國民軍

例：Ironically, the whole society relied on the militia for food and daily supplies. 諷刺的是，整個社會所需之食物與日常用品是依賴民兵提供的。

❺ demilitarized ▶ de(not) + militarized

adj. 非軍事化的，非武裝的

例：After the war, we have many demilitarized areas in this neighborhood. 戰後，此區有非常多解除軍備區。

Part1｜人體&社會

man、mani、manu 手

❶ manage ▸ man(hand) + age

v. 控制，經營，管理，設法

例：Can you teach me how to manage my monthly budget?
你可以教我如何管理每月預算嗎？

❷ manifest ▸ mani(hand) + fest（侵擾 = strike）

adj. 顯然的，明顯的 v. 顯示，表達

例：His theory manifested a particular viewpoint into the way of life.
他的理論展示出一種對生命之道的獨特見解。

❸ manipulate ▸ mani + pul（充滿）+ ate

v. 操縱，操控

例：She's trying to manipulate you. Can't you see?
你看不出來她正在操控你嗎？

❹ manual ▸ manu + al

adj. 手的，手工的 n. 手冊，小冊子

例：Read the manual carefully before you operate this machine.
在操控這台機器之前，詳閱手冊。

❺ manufactory ▸ manu + fact（做 = make）+ ory（地方）

n. 製造廠，工廠

例：Our manager asked us to visit the manufactory twice a month.
我們的經理要求我們每個月要造訪工廠兩次。

nerv、neuro 神經

❶ nervous ▸ nerv + ous

adj. 神經的，緊張不安的

例：I usually get quite nervous before making a public speech.
在演講之前，我總是會變得非常緊張。

❷ unnerve ▸ un(not) + nerve

v. 使失去力氣，身心俱疲，使焦躁

例：This unnerving experience makes me no longer like to eat meat.
這個令人緊張不安的經驗讓我不再喜歡吃肉。

❸ neural ▸ neur + al →神經的

adj. 神經的，神經中樞的

例：Neural systems enable us to savor each sensorial experience.
神經系統使我們能細細品嚐每個感官經驗。

❹ neurology ▸ neur + ology（研究）

n. 神經學，神經病學

例：As a medical student, I'm highly interested in neurology.
身為一名醫學生，我對神經學有高度興趣。

❺ neurosis ▸ neuro + sis

n. 神經機能病，神經衰弱症

例：Depressive neurosis is getting more and more common. We have to do something about it.
抑鬱型精神官能症愈趨常見。我們必須採取行動。

nat 出生

❶ natal ▸ nat(born) + al

adj. 出生的，誕生的

例：According to the law, pre-natal leaves should be granted without any reasons. 根據法條，應毫無理由給予產前假。

❷ nation ▸ nat(born) + ion

n. 國家

例：We're lucky to be born in this nation called Taiwan.
我們都有幸能出生在這個名叫台灣的國家。

❸ native ▸ nat + ive

adj. 本國的，本地的，與生俱來的

例：This position only hire native English speakers.
這個職缺只雇用英語母語人士。

❹ nature ▸ nat(born) + ure

n. 自然，天然，天性

例：Craving for a better life is human nature.
想要擁有更好的生活是人類的天性。

❺ innate ▸ in(into) + nate(be born)

adj. 與生俱來的，先天的，固有的

例：His innate sentimentality has caused him much trouble in looking for a job. 他先天的善感讓他求職不順。

ped 腳

❶ peddle ▶ ped + dle

v. 沿街叫賣，兜售，散播

例：The vendor peddled along the main street.
小販沿著大街叫賣。

❷ pedicure ▶ pedi + cure（照護）

n./v. 修腳趾甲

例：Many housewives like to gossip when getting a pedicure.
許多家庭主婦喜歡在做腳趾甲護理的時候聊八卦。

❸ pedestrian ▶ pedes + tr + ian

n. 行人

例：The car accidentally hit the pedestrians on the sidewalk.
車子不小心撞上人行道上的行人。

❹ expedient ▶ ex(out) + ped + ient

adj. 方便的，權宜的，有益的

例：We can view of this tentative proposal as an expedient one.
我們可以將此暫時性方案當作一權宜之計。

❺ centipede ▶ centi（百 = hundred）+ pede

n. 蜈蚣

例：After the traumatic experience, I'm terrified at the sight of a centipede.
在這個創傷性的經驗之後，只要看到蜈蚣我就會感到很害怕。

popul、publ 人們

❶ populace ▸ popul(people) + ace

n. 大眾，平民，人口

例：These votes only accounted for a small part of the populace.
這些票數只代表全體人口的一小部分。

❷ popular ▸ popul(people) + ar

adj. 受歡迎的，流行的

例：Our newest serum is very popular among young girls now.
我們最新的精華液現在很受年輕女孩歡迎。

❸ populate ▸ popul + ate

v. 居住於

例：The terrain is heavily populated by daffodils. 水仙大量繁衍於此地。

❹ public ▸ publ + ic

adj. 公眾的，公用的 n. 公眾，社會，公共場合

例：You should wear masks in public spaces.
在公眾場合你應該戴口罩。

❺ publish ▸ publ + ish

v. 發表，公佈，發行

例：The popular writer just published her second novel last month.
這位受歡迎的作家上個月剛發行她第二本小說。

Part1 | 人體&社會

psych 心理、精神

❶ psyche ▸ psyche(mind)

n. 靈魂，心智

例：Human psyche is complex and unable to dichotomize.
人類心智是複雜且無法被二分的。

❷ psychedelic ▸ psyche + del（顯示） + ic

n. 迷幻劑 adj. 引起幻覺的

例：Many famous writers and filmmakers took psychedelic when they were young. 許多知名作家和導演在年輕時皆食用過迷幻藥。

❸ psychology ▸ psych + ology（研究）

n. 心理學

例：Studying psychology doesn't necessarily make you a good psychologist. 讀心理學並不一定會讓你成為一名好的心理師。

❹ psychoanalysis ▸ psycho + analysis（分析）

n. 精神分析（學）

例：Psychoanalysis is considered by some as outdated.
精神分析被部分人視為過時。

❺ psychotherapy ▸ psycho + therapy（治療 = cure）

n. 精神療法，心理療法

例：If counseling doesn't work, maybe you can try psychotherapy.
如果諮商沒有用，也許你可以試試看精神療法。

Part1 | 人體&社會

soci 群體

❶ social ▸ soci(join) + al

adj. 社會的，社交的，社會性的

例：I personally dislike social activities. I find it tiresome and boring.
我個人不喜歡社交活動。我覺得很累人且無聊。

❷ society ▸ soci + ety（名詞字尾）

n. 社會，社會集團，共同體

例：Living in a democratic society enables me to have freedom of speech. 住在民主社會讓我得以擁有言論自由。

❸ sociology ▸ soci + ology（研究）

n. 社會學

例：I wish I had chosen sociology as my major. I want to know more about its structure.
我希望我當初有選社會學當作主修。我想要更瞭解其架構。

❹ associate ▸ as(to) + soci + ate

v. 聯合，連結 adj. 聯合的 n. 夥伴

例：I found it rather hard to associate the cores of these two theories.
我發現要連結這兩個理論的核心相當困難。

❺ dissociate ▸ dis(away) + soci + ate

v. 使分離，分開

例：You need to dissociate your personal opinions from facts before you make fair judgement.
在進行公正判斷之前，你必須先將個人評論與事實區分開來。

Part1 | 人體&社會

viv、vit 生命

❶ vital ▸ vit(live) + al

adj. 生命的，有活力的，極其重要的 n. 重要的部分，重要器官

例：Keeping a work-life balance is of vital importance.
維持工作與生活平衡是極其重要的。

❷ vivacious ▸ viv + ac(y) + ious

adj. 有活力的，活潑的

例：He's always open-minded and vivacious. No wonder everyone wants to be friends with him.
他總是開明又充滿活力。難怪每個人都想和他做朋友。

❸ vivid ▸ viv(live) + id（形容詞字尾）

adj. 朝氣蓬勃的，生動的，栩栩如生的

例：This painting finely presents the vivid rural life in the 50s.
這幅畫完美地呈現出五零年代生氣蓬勃的農村生活。

❹ revive ▸ re(again) + vive(live)

v. 使甦醒，使復活，使恢復，使復興

例：I'm sure shoulder pads will revive in the years to come.
我相信幾年後墊肩會再度流行。

❺ survive ▸ sur(over) + vive(live)

v. 生存

例：Can any of us survive in a war?
我們之中有人能在戰爭中存活下來嗎？

path、pass 感覺

❶ passion ▸ pass(feeling) + ion

n. 熱情

例：Modern people are losing passion in almost everything now.
現代人對所有事物幾乎都失去熱情了。

❷ compassion ▸ com + passion

n. 憐憫，同情

例：Would you please show just a little bit of compasison to the homeless man? 你能不能就施捨一點同情給那名無家可歸的男子？

❸ pathetic ▸ path(feeling) + et + ic

adj. 可憐的，悲哀的，可悲的

例：She's so pathetic. All she can do is gossiping around.
她真可悲，只會四處八卦。

❹ apathy ▸ a(not) + pathy

n. 冷漠，無興趣，漠不關心

例：He listened to the speech with apathy and left right after it ended.
他漠不關心地聽著演講，並在結束後馬上離去。

❺ sympathy ▸ sym(together) + pathy

n. 同情，同理

例：I often harbor great sympathy toward underdogs.
我總是對不得志的人懷以巨大同情。

sens、sent 感覺

❶ sensation ▸ sens(feel) + ation

n. 感覺，轟動一時的人（或事物），激動

例：The album was a sensatio n. You couldn't even imagine.
這張唱片當時轟動一時。你根本無法想像。

❷ sensible ▸ sens(feel) + ible（可以的）

adj. 明智的，合乎情理的

例：He just couldn't make a sensible decision even when we told him the truth. 即便我們已告訴他真相，他仍然無法做出一個明智的決定。

❸ sensitive ▸ sens(feel) + I + tive

adj. 敏感的，易受影響的

例：My skin is highly sensitive to any products containing acid.
我的肌膚對酸性產品非常敏感。

❹ sensual ▸ sens + ual

adj. 滿足於感官的，耽於酒色的

例：Sensual satisfaction doesn't last long. 感官愉悅無法長久。

❺ sentiment ▸ senti(feel) + ment

n. 感情，情緒，心情

例：Such sentiment can only be felt by sensitive people.
只有敏感的人才能感受到這種情緒。

❻ consent ▸ con(together) + sent

v./n. 同意，認可（= agree to opinions）

例：My parents did not consent to my idea of going abroad this month.
我爸媽不同意我想要這個月出國的想法。

❼ dissent ▸ dis(away) + sent

v./n. 意見不同，提出異議

例：The project was agreed upon without any dissent.
此專案毫無異議，予以通過。

❽ resent ▸ re（對抗 = against）+ sent(feel)

v. 憤慨，怨恨

例：I resent his pretentiousness to the point where I don't want to see him. 我討厭他的自視甚高，已到了不想看見他的程度。

❾ consensus ▸ con(together) + sens + us

n. （意見等）一致

例：After ten hours of meeting, we finally reach a consensus.
在十小時的會議後，我們終於達成了共識。

❿ sentient ▸ sent(feel) + ient

adj. 有感覺能力的，可以感覺的 n. 有知覺的人

例：All living beings are sentient and we shouldn't harm them willfully.
所有生物都是有知覺能力的，我們不應恣意傷害他們。

cap、capit 頭

❶ capable ▸ cap(head) + able（能夠的）

adj. 有能力的，有才能的，能夠勝任的

例：I am not sure if I am capable of managing this project.
我不確定我是否能勝任管理此項專案。

❷ capital ▸ capit(head) + al

adj. 首要的，大寫字母的，可處以死刑的 n. 首都，大寫字母，資本

例：Capital punishment is still under heated debate right now.
死刑現在仍遭受激烈爭議。

❸ captain ▸ capt(head) + ain

n. 首領，（陸軍、空軍）上尉，海軍上校，機長 v. 指揮

例：He used to be the captain of this giant vessel.
他曾是這輛超大戰艦的船長。

❹ captivate ▸ cap(head) + tiv + ate

v. 迷惑，迷住

例：I was captivated by his sophistication and talent.
我深受他的世故與才華吸引。

❺ capture ▸ capt(head) + ure

v. 捕獲，獲得 n. 捕獲，戰利品，俘虜

例：I only captured three snakes in the hunting competition.
在狩獵比賽中我只捕獲三條蛇。

Part 2｜五官動作

audi、audit 聽

❶ audible ▶ aud(hear) + ible（可以的）

adj. 能聽到的，聽得見的

例：Some animals create sounds that are not audible to the human ears. 有些動物會發出人類耳朵聽不到的聲音。

❷ audience ▶ aud(hear) + i + ence

n. 聽眾，觀眾，讀者

例：The audience was applauding for the amazing performance.
觀眾正在為精彩的表演鼓掌。

❸ audit ▶ audit(hear)

n./v. 審計

例：The audit process usually take a long time, so you need to prepare the files in advance.
審計程序通常需要花很長的時間，所以你需要事先把資料準備好。

❹ auditor ▶ audit + or（表示人的字尾）

n. 聽者，旁聽者，審計員

例：The auditor suspected that our company didn't pay taxes.
審計員懷疑我們公司逃稅。

❺ auditorium ▶ auditor + ium（表示地點）

n. 聽眾席，講堂，禮堂

例：The auditorium was packed with athletes for the annual sports event. 禮堂因為年度運動賽事充滿了運動員。

face 臉；面

❶ deface ▶ de（表否定）+ face

v. 損傷外觀，污損

例：The acid deface the fine wood, and my mom was really angry.
酸損壞了高級木頭的表面，我媽媽非常生氣。

❷ efface ▶ ef(out) + face

v. 消除，抹去

例：The medicine was claimed to have the power to efface all traumatic memories. 這種藥據說可以消除所有創傷回憶。

❸ preface ▶ pre(before) + face

n. 序言，引語 v. 作序

例：My dad added a preface into the book before he published it.
在書上市之前，我爸爸多加了一個序言。

❹ surface ▶ sur(out) + face

n. 表面，外觀 v. 浮出水面，呈現，加上表面

例：Oil floats on the surface of the water, and we all refused to drink it.
油浮在水的表面上，我們都拒絕喝它。

❺ interface ▶ inter(between) + face

n. 交界面，介面 v. 連接

例：The website has a really user-friendly interface, even for the elderly. 這個網站介面非常容易上手，就連對老年人來說也一樣。

Part 2｜五官動作

ocul、opth 眼睛

❶ ocular ▶ ocul(eye) + ar

adj. 視覺的，眼睛的 n. 目鏡

例：Serious ocular diseases usually take a long time to recover.
嚴重的眼疾通常需要花長時間恢復。

❷ monocle ▶ mon(one) + ocle(eye)

n. 單片眼鏡，單眼鏡

例：Wearing a monocle is viewed by some as fashionable.
帶單片眼鏡被某些人視為是流行的。

❸ binocular ▶ bi(two) + nocul + ar

n. 雙筒望遠鏡

例：This binocular is expensive, so it's usually purchased by the government for academic use.
這個雙筒望遠鏡很昂貴，所以通常都是政府購買做學術研究。

❹ inoculate ▶ in(into) + ocul + ate

v. （醫）預防接種，灌輸

例：The doctor inoculated my brother against the flu.
醫生替我的弟弟注射流感預防針。

❺ ophthalmologist

▶ ophthalm(eye) + olog(y) + ist（表示人的字尾）

n. 眼科醫師

例：Ironically, most of the ophthalmologist do not take good care of their eyes. 諷刺的是，許多眼科醫生並沒有好好照護自己的眼睛。

Part 2｜五官動作

rhino、nas 鼻

❶ rhinoceros ▸ rhino + cer（角 = horn） + os

n. 犀牛

例：We went to the zoo to see the rhinoceros and the famous pandas.
我們去動物園看犀牛，以及鼎鼎大名的熊貓。

❷ rhinology ▸ rhino + (o)logy（研究）

n. 鼻科學

例：Rhinology is relatively a less popular major.
鼻科學相對來說是冷門主修。

❸ rhinoplasty ▸ rhino + plasty（整形術）

n. 整鼻形術

例：Now, many men undergo rhinoplasty as well.
現今，許多男性也會進行整鼻手術。

❹ nasal ▸ nas(nose) + al

adj. 鼻的，鼻音的

例：Nasal sounds are hard to pronounce for people who speak languages from another linguistic system.
對於使用其他語言系統的人來說，鼻音很難發。

❺ nasitis ▸ nas(nose) + itis（發言= inflammation）

n. 鼻炎

例：The medication for my grandfather's nasitis isn't working.
我爺爺的鼻炎藥沒有效果。

Part 2｜五官動作

vid、vis 看

❶ video ▸ vid + eo

n. 影片，錄影帶 adj. 電視的，影像的

例：Let's watch the video that's going viral on Facebook.
我們來看在臉書上瘋傳的影片吧。

❷ visible ▸ vis(look) + ible（可以的）

adj. 看得見的

例：The man was barely visible in the dark. 男子在黑暗中難以被查覺。

❸ vision ▸ vis(look) + ion（名詞字尾）

n. 視力，洞察力，先見之明

例：I have a poor vision and such phenomenon is diagnosed as genetic.
我的視力不好，且診斷為遺傳性現象。

❹ visual ▸ vis(look) + ual

adj. 視覺的，視力的，看得見的

例：Near-sightedness and far-sightedness are both visual defects.
近視和遠視都屬視力缺陷。

❺ evidence ▸ e(out) + vid + ence

n. 證據 v. 證明，顯示

例：Please exhibit your evidence for the charge.
請上呈訴訟證據。

voc、vok 呼喊

❶ vocal ▶ voc(call) + al

adj. 聲音的，口頭的，有聲的

例：I hired a vocal coach to improve my singing skills.
我請了一名聲音指導老師，進而改善我的唱歌技巧。

❷ vocation ▶ voc(call) + ation（名詞字尾）

n. 職業，天職，天命

例：Teaching is my vocation, and I also earn a lot of money from it.
教書是我的天命，我也從中賺了不少錢。

❸ avocation ▶ a(away) + voc + ation

n. 副業，興趣，業餘愛好

例：Painting is just my avocation. I don't take it seriously.
畫畫只是我的業餘愛好，我沒有認真看待。

❹ advocate ▶ ad(to) + voc + ate

v. 主張，提倡，擁護 n. 擁護者，宣導者，律師

例：My dad, interestingly, is a strong advocate for feminism.
很有趣的是，我爸爸大力擁護女性主義。

❺ evoke ▶ e(out) + voke

v. 引起，喚起

例：The sketch evoked wistful memories in me.
這幅草圖勾起了我心中惆悵的回憶。

❻ invoke ▶ in(into) + voke

v. 祈禱，懇請，召喚

例：It is said that the witch invoked evil spirits to get revenge.
據說那名女巫召喚惡靈進行報復。

❼ provoke ▶ pro(forth) + voke

v. 惹起，激怒，刺激

例：Why don't you stop provoking the homeless man?
你為何不停止激怒那名無家可歸的男子？

❽ revoke ▶ re(again) + voke

v. 撤回，取消，廢除

例：If you don't want to get your driver's license revoked, abide by the law. 如果你不想要駕照被吊銷，就遵守法律。

❾ convoke ▶ con(together) + voke

v. 召集……開會，召集

例：The president convoked Parliament and declared national emergency right away.
總統召集國會，且隨即宣佈國家緊急狀態。

❿ irrevocable

▶ ir(not) + re(again) + voc + able（可以的）

adj. 不可改變的，不能取消的

例：The decision is irrevocable, so getting down to business is only alternative. 這項決策是無法撤回的，所以趕快做事是唯一的選擇。

Part 2 | 五官動作

vo(u)r、ed 吃

❶ devour ▸ de(down) + vour(eat)

v. 狼吞虎嚥，吞食

例：The wolf devour the body of the deer right away.
狼馬上就把鹿的屍體吞食掉了。

❷ carnivore ▸ carni（肉 = flesh）+ vore(eat)

n. 肉食性動物

例：Both lions and tigers are carnivores living on the plain.
獅子和老虎都是生活在草原上的肉食性動物。

❸ herbivorous ▸ herbi（植物 = plant）+ vor + ous

adj. 食草的

例：Most birds are herbivorous and rely heavily on water.
大多數的鳥都是草食性的，且大量依賴水為生。

❹ omnivorous ▸ omni（全部的 = all）+ vor + ous

adj. 雜食的，興趣廣泛的

例：Human beings are omnivorous, but going vegan is a thing now.
人類是雜食性動物，但是現在正流行吃全素。

❺ edible ▸ ed(eat) + ible（可以的）

adj. 可食用的，可吃的 n. 食品

例：Plastic is not edible. Keep it out of children's reach.
塑膠不能吃，要放在小孩拿不到的地方。

log、loq 說話

❶ logic ▸ log + ic

n. 邏輯

例：Your logic doesn't make any sense. Please reframe your statement. 你的邏輯不合理。請重述論述。

❷ colloquial ▸ col（共同的）+ loqu + ial

n. 口語的

例：This is a colloquial slang; you can learn it to sound more like a native speaker. 這是口語俗諺，你可以學起來，聽起來會更像母語人士。

❸ prologue ▸ pro（往前的）+ log + ue

n. 序言，開場白 v. 作序，念開場白

例：The prologue of the play is really well-written.
這齣戲的前言寫的真的非常好。

❹ dialogue ▸ dia(through) + log + ue

n. 對話

例：Practice dialogue one before you proceed to the writing exercise.
在進行寫作練習之前，先練習對話一。

❺ monologue ▸ mono(one) + log + ue

n. 獨白

例：The monologues in all Shakespeare's plays convey thought-provoking messages.
在莎士比亞的所有戲劇裡，每個獨白都傳達了發人省思的訊息。

Part 3｜方位時間

ann-、enn- 年

❶ anniversary ▶ anni + vers（轉 = turn）+ ary

n. 紀念日 adj. 每年的，每一年的

例：Today is my parent's 20th anniversary.
今天是我爸媽的二十週年紀念日。

❷ annual ▶ ann + ual

adj. 一年的，年度的 n. 年刊

例：The annual year-end meeting is going to be held on 29th, December. 年度年終會議將在十二月二十九號舉行。

❸ biannual ▶ bi(two) + annual

adj. 一年兩次的

例：This is a biannual magazine and the subscription fees are very low.
這是一年發行兩次的雜誌，訂閱費用很低。

❹ millennial ▶ mill(thousand) + enn(year) + ial

adj. 一千年的 n. 千禧世代

例：Millennials tend to be more pessimistic.
千禧世代通常都比較悲觀和消極。

❺ perennial

▶ per（徹底的 = completely）+ enn(year) + ial

adj. 終年的，長期存在的，多年生的 n. 多年生植物

例：Our company has been suffering from perennial shortage of raw materials. 我們公司苦惱於原物料的長期短缺。

Part 3 | 方位時間

center、centr 中心

❶ centralize ▸ centr + al + ize（動詞字尾）

v. 集中，使……中心（央）化

例：The CEO wants to centralize all shipping and packaging operations in one single factory.
總裁希望能將運輸和包裝作業全部集中至單一工廠。

❷ concentrate ▸ con（一起 = together）+ centr + ate

v. 全神貫注，專注

例：I want you to concentrate in the final exam so you don't get flunked twice. 我要你專注在期末考上，你才不會被當兩次。

❸ eccentric ▸ ec(out) + centr + ic

adj. 古怪的，異常的

例：He wears eccentric clothes all the time, even when he's doing shopping. 他總是穿著怪異，甚至連購物時都一樣。

❹ epicenter ▸ epi(upon) + center

n. 震央，中心

例：The epicenter of the earthquake is located in Taitung.
此地震的震央在台東。

❺ geocentric ▸ geo（地球 = earth）+ centr + ic

adj. 以地球為中心的

例：The geocentric theory of the universe has already been debunked.
宇宙的地球中心論早已被破解。

chron 時間

❶ chronic ▸ chron + ic

adj. 慢性的，長期的，不斷的

例：People suffering from chronic diseases are subjected to delayed full recovery. 患有慢性病的人康復時間會延長。

❷ chronicle ▸ chron + ic + le

n. 年代記，編年史 v. 載入編年史

例：Go to the museum on the corner to check on the chronicle of the October Revolution. 到轉角那間博物館查閱十月革命史。

❸ chronology ▸ chron + ology（研究）

n. 年代記，年代學，年表

例：The chronology of the dynasty took a long time to complete.
該朝代的年代記花了很長的時間才完成。

❹ synchronize ▸ syn（一起的）+ chron + ize

v. 同時發生

例：Can you possibly synchronize this two machines so we can get the result faster? 你能同步這兩台機器，以便我們更快取得結果嗎？

❺ chronological ▸ chrono + log(y) + ical

adj. 按年月順序的

例：The files were organized in chronological order, so it's easy to track.
檔案是按年月順序整理的，這樣方便追蹤。

number、numer 數字

❶ outnumber ▶ out + number

v. 在數量上超過，比……多

例：The enemy certainly outnumbered us in this battle.
在此場戰役中，敵軍人數確實比我們的多。

❷ numeral ▶ numer + al

n. 數字 adj. 數位的，表示數位的

例：Roman numerals can still be seen in certain historical records.
羅馬數字仍然可以在某些歷史紀錄中被看見。

❸ numerous ▶ numer + ous（形容詞字尾）

adj. 許多的，很多的

例：Numerous athletes took part in this competition for the second time. 許多運動員都是第二次參加此場競賽。

❹ enumerate ▶ e(out) + numer + ate

v. 列舉，計算

例：Please enumerate 1 to 10 in Japanese one by one.
請一個接著一個用日文念出一到十。

❺ innumerable ▶ in（表否定）+ numer + able（可以的）

adj. 無數的，數不清的

例：Innumerable stars shine in the sky. 無數星星在天空中閃爍。

meter、metr 測量

❶ diameter ▸ dia（通過 = through）+ meter

n. 直徑

例：Measure the diameter of the circle first. 請先將該圓的直徑測量出來。

❷ geometry ▸ geo（土地 = earth）+ metry

n. 幾何學

例：Geometry is incomprehensible for me. That's why I always failed it in high school.
幾何學對我來說超出理解範圍。這就是為什麼我高中總是被當。

❸ symmetry ▸ sym(same) + metry

n. 對稱性，整齊，勻稱

例：The perfect symmetry of the floral pattern on the embroidery fascinated me. 刺繡品上花朵完美的對稱讓我著迷。

❹ asymmetry ▸ a（表否定）+ sym + metry

n. 不對稱

例：The asymmetry of the circle makes me want to re-draw it again.
圓的不對稱讓我想要重新再畫一遍。

❺ centimeter ▸ cent（百 = hundred）+ i + meter

n. 公分

例：The unit of the measurement is centimeter. 測量單位是公分。

Part 3 | 方位時間

seque、secut 跟隨

❶ sequel ▶ sequ + el

n. 繼續，結果，歸結，（故事，電影等的）續集

例：I'm dying to see the sequel of the film!
我等不及要看這部電影的續集了！

❷ sequent ▶ sequ + ent

adj. 其次的，連續的，作為結果發生的

例：The event is sequent to the outbreak of the terrifying disease.
此事件是接續著可怕病毒爆發後發生的。

❸ consequent ▶ con（一起的 = together）+ sequent

adj. 隨之發生的

例：I'll back you up on this, but you should beware the consequent aftermath. 在這件事情上我會支持你，但你要注意隨之發生的後果。

❹ prosecute ▶ pro（向前的 = forth）+ secute

v. 起訴，執行

例：We all hope the government can prosecute the man in the random-killing case as soon as possible.
我們都希望政府可以盡快起訴這此隨機殺人案件中的男子。

❺ subsequent ▶ sub（之下 = under）+ sequent

adj. 今後的，隨之而來的

例：In the subsequent chapters, we'll see how the plot develops.
在接下來的章節中，我們會看到情節如何發展。

Part 3｜方位時間

tempo 時間

❶ temporal ▸ tempor + al

adj. 時間的，暫時的，世俗的 n. 世間事物

例：All living forms are temporal beings, and we should cherish everything we have. 所有生命體都是短暫存在的，我們都應珍惜我們擁有的事物。

❷ contemporaneous

▸ con（一起的 = together）+ tempor + aneous

adj. 同時代的

例：Shakespeare and J. K. Rowling are certainly not contemporaneous.
莎士比亞和 J. K. 羅琳一定不是同時代的人。

❸ contemporary ▸ con + tempor + ary

adj. 當代的，同時代的 n. 同時代的人

例：Haruki Murakami is a contemporary Japanese writer.
村上春樹是當代日本作家。

❹ extemporal ▸ ex(out) + tempor + al

adj. 即時的，無準備的

例：Extemporal wit is highly essential for stand-up comedians.
即席的機智對於脫口秀喜劇演員來說非常重要。

❺ spatiotemporal ▸ spatio(space) + tempor + al

adj. 空間和時間上的，時空的

例：It's imperative that you observe the spatiotemporal settings in each historical event. 在觀察每個歷史事件時，注意時空背景是至關重要的。

Part 4｜一般行為

act、ag 行動、做

❶ active ▸ act + ive（形容詞字尾）

adj. 活躍的，現行的，積極的 n. 積極份子

例：My father is an active member of the organization.
我爸爸是此組織的活躍成員。

❷ activate ▸ act + iv(e) + ate（使）

v. 啟動，活化

例：This chemical will activate the synthesis process.
這個化學藥物會啟動合成過程。

❸ counteract ▸ counter(against) + act

v. 對抗，抵制，抵消，中和

例：The act basically counteracted our long-term efforts on labor issues.
此法案基本上抵消了我們長期對於勞工議題的努力。

❹ enact ▸ en（使） + act

v. 制定法律，扮演（某種角色）

例：We should enact a law that protects labors as soon as possible.
我們應盡快制定一項保障勞工的法律。

❺ interact ▸ inter（之間 = between） + act

v. 相互作用，互動

例：Remember to interact with the guests and make them feel like home. 記得要和客人互動，讓他們覺得賓至如歸。

❻ exact ▸ ex(out) + act

adj. 精確的，精密的 v. 強求，要求

例：Without exact estimations on the economic prospect, our company will go bankrupt.

若沒有對於經濟前景的準確預測，我們的公司將會破產。

❼ react ▸ re(back) + act

v. 反應，起作用，起化學反應

例：Why did you reacted this way? Were you offended?

你為什麼會有這樣的反應？你覺得被冒犯了嗎？

❽ agent ▸ ag + ent

n. 代理人，仲介人，代表，媒介

例：Lily is my agent, so you need to contact her for more cooperation details.

莉莉是我的經紀人，所以你需要和她聯絡以取得更多合作細節。

❾ agile ▸ ag(do) + ile（形容詞字尾）

adj. 動作敏捷的，機敏的

例："As agile as a hare" is a phrase to describe one's movement or personality.

「像狡兔一樣機敏」是拿來形容一個人的動作和個性的片語。

❿ agitate ▸ ag + it(go) + ate

v. 激起，煽動

例：The police's oppression further agitated the crowd.

警方的鎮壓更加激怒的群眾。

Part 4｜一般行為

amble、ambul 走

❶ ambulance ▶ ambul + ance（名詞字尾）

n. 救護車

例：Take her onto the ambulance for emergency treatment!
把她抬上就救護車做緊急治療！

❷ ambulate ▶ ambul + ate

v. 走動，移動

例：After careful treatment, the elderly is able to ambulate for a short distance. 在細心的治療後，老人已經可以短距離行走了。

❸ circumambulate

▶ circum（周圍 = around）+ ambul + ate

v. 巡行，試探

例：They will carry the torches and circumambulate the stadium.
他們會手持聖火，繞競技場一圈。

❹ preamble ▶ pre（先前 = before）+ amble

n. 前言，序言

例：The preamble of the book states clearly the purpose of the research. 這本書的序言清楚地說明了研究的目的。

❺ somnambulism ▶ somn（睡眠）+ ambul + ism

n. 夢遊

例：My brother finally got rid of somnambulism after 3 years of treatment. 在治療三年後，我弟弟終於不再夢遊了。

Part 4｜一般行為

acr、acu 尖銳的

❶ acrid ▸ acr + id

adj. 刺鼻的，（行為、態度、語言等）刻薄的

例：The acrid smell of the dish made me lost appetite at once.
餐點刺鼻的味道讓我頓失胃口。

❷ acrimony ▸ acri + mony（表狀態）

n. 辛辣，刻薄

例：I wouldn't harbor any acrimony toward him despite his rude remarks. 儘管他說了無理的話，我也不會對他惡言相向。

❸ acuity ▸ acu + ity（名詞字尾）

n. 敏銳，尖銳，劇烈

例：Hearing acuity usually declined during the aging process.
聽覺的敏銳度通常歲隨著老化過程降低。

❹ acute ▸ acu + te（後綴形容詞字尾）

adj. 急性的，非常嚴重的，敏銳的

例：This acute budge problem should be resolved by the end of the day. 此嚴重的預算問題要在今天結束前解決。

❺ acupuncture ▸ acu + punct（刺） + ure

n. 針灸

例：My mother recommend me acupuncture for my back pain.
我媽媽推薦我去針灸治療背痛。

auc、aux、aug 增加

❶ auction ▶ auct + ion（名詞字尾）

n. 拍賣 v. 競賣

例：The painting "self-destroyed" right after it was sold in the auction.
這幅畫在拍賣會中售出之後立即「自毀」。

❷ augment ▶ aug + ment（名詞字尾）

v. 增加，提高

例：The report augmented the already-rising panic in the public.
報導增加了早在提升的大眾恐慌。

❸ auxiliary ▶ aux + ili + ary

adj. 輔助的，協助的，預備的 n. 輔助工具，附屬組織

例：The auxiliary equipment will help you hear better.
此輔助設備能幫助你的聽力。

❹ august ▶ aug + ust

adj. 令人敬畏的，尊嚴的

例：The august and magnificent historical building makes me want to stay a bit longer. 高大又壯觀的歷史建物讓我想再多待久一點。

❺ auxin ▶ aux + in（事物）

n. 生長素

例：Farmers rarely use auxins for plant-growing nowadays.
農夫們現今很少使用生長素來種植植物了。

Part 4｜一般行為

ceive、cept 拿取

❶ accept ▸ ac(to) + cept

v. 接受，同意，答應

例：I don't see why you should refuse to accept this offer.
我想不到任何你應該拒絕接受此邀約的理由。

❷ conceive ▸ con（一同 = with） + ceive

v. 構思，懷孕

例：We spent the whole afternoon conceiving the draft of the blueprint.
我們花了一下午的時間構思藍圖的草稿。

❸ deceive ▸ de(down) + ceive

v. 欺騙，欺瞞

例：By making this statement, the government is apparently deceiving the citizen. 做出此番發言，政府很顯然是在欺騙人民。

❹ except ▸ ex(out) + cept

v. 除外，除了

例：We'll all go to the field trip, except Mandy and Jonas.
我們全部都會參加戶外教學，除了曼蒂和強納斯。

❺ intercept ▸ inter（之間 = between） + cept

v./n. 攔截，中斷

例：The missile was immediately intercepted by our army.
飛彈快速由我方軍隊攔截。

❻ perceive ▸ per（完全地 = completely） + ceive

v. 感知，認知，理解

例：It's all about how you perceive the world and how you decide to interact with others.

問題全在於你如何感知世界以及如何與他人互動。

❼ precept ▸ pre（先前的 = before） + cept

n. 訓誡，格言，命令書，令狀

例：Islamic precepts are to be firmly conformed to without any reasons.

伊斯蘭教的戒律應毫無其他理由強力遵守。

❽ receive ▸ re(again) + ceive

v. 獲得，收到，得到，受到

例：I finally received the scholarship after months of waiting.

在幾個月的等待之後，我終於領到獎學金了。

❾ inception ▸ in(into) + cept + ion（名詞字尾）

n. 開始，開端

例：The inception of the whole chaos was rooted from the politician's ignorant remark.

這整場紛擾的開端始於該名政客無知的發言。

❿ susceptible ▸ sus(under) + cept + ible

adj. 善感的，敏感的，易受……影響的

例：This medication will cure the disease, but it'll also make you susceptible to sunlight hereafter.

藥物會治癒此疾病，但也會讓你從今以後對陽光敏感。

Part 4｜一般行為

cad、cas、cid 掉落

❶ accident ▸ ac(to) + cid + ent

n. 意外，偶發事件

例：Three men died in the terrible car accident.
三名男子死於這場可怕的車禍。

❷ cascade ▸ cas + cade →小的

n. 小瀑布，瀑布之流，一連串的事物 v. 像瀑布般留下，使成一串

例：We drove for two hours to appreciate the beautiful cascade.
我們開了兩個小時的車去溪賞美麗的小瀑布。

❸ decadent ▸ de(down) + cad + ent

adj. 衰退的，墮落的 n. 頹廢的人

例：The decadent aristocracy basically seeded their own downfall.
墮落的貴族基本上一手造成了自己的失敗。

❹ incident ▸ in(into) + cid(fall) + ent

n. 事件 adj. 易發的

例：The 911 incident still triggered lots of sentiments from the society.
社會對於 911 事件仍心有所感。

❺ casual ▸ cas + ual

adj. 偶然的，平常的 n. 休閒服

例：Let's make it casual and see where things take us.
我們就隨性點吧，視情況行動。

cise 切割

❶ concise ▶ con（一起的 = together） + cise

adj. 簡潔的，簡要的

例：Our professor asked us to make a concise summary of the paper in ten minutes. 我們教授要求我們在十分鐘內替這份論文做簡潔的摘要。

❷ decide ▶ de(down) + cide

v. 決定

例：I decided not to be friends with him anymore.
我決定不要再和他當朋友了。

❸ exorcise ▶ exor（向外 = out） + cise

v. 驅鬼，消災

例：In the film, the man exorcised the evil spirit for the little girl.
在電影中，男子替小女孩驅魔。

❹ incise ▶ in（向內 = into） + cise

v. 切割，切斷，刻

例：The blacksmith incised a totem into the product and it came out pretty well. 鐵匠將圖騰刻入產品之中，成品相當好。

❺ precise ▶ pre（先前的 = before） + cise

adj. 準確的，精確的

例：I need precise figures, or you are fired.
我需要準確的數據，不然你就被開除了。

Part 4｜一般行為

cide 殺

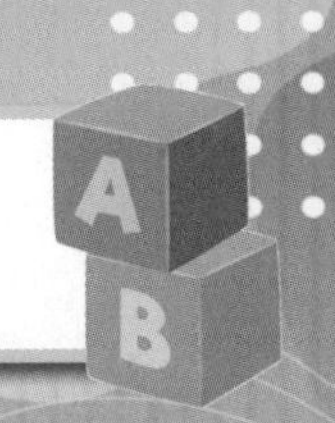

❶ homicide ▸ homi（人）+ cide

n. 殺人

例：The man committed homicide and was sentenced for 30 years.
男子犯了殺人罪，被判三十年有期徒刑。

❷ genocide ▸ geno（總族 = race）+ cide

n. 種族滅絕，種族屠殺

例：The heart-wrenching genocide was certainly an event we avoid to repeat. 此令人心痛的種族屠殺絕對是我們不想再重新經歷的事件。

❸ regicide ▸ reg（治理）+ i + cide

n. 弒君

例：The theme of regicide is common in Shakespeare's plays.
弒君的主題在莎士比亞的劇本中很常見。

❹ insecticide ▸ insecti（昆蟲）+ cide

n. 殺蟲劑（= pesticide）

例：Many types of insecticides are banned due to public opinions.
因公眾輿論，許多種殺蟲劑已經被禁止使用了。

❺ suicide ▸ sui（自我 = self）+ cide

n. 自殺（行為）

例：I hope suicide can be less commonly-seen in modern society.
我希望在現今社會中，自殺能越來越少見。

ced、cess、ceed 行走

❶ incessant ▸ in(not) + cess + ant

adj. 不停的，不斷的

例：The incessant questions from the little boy finally angered his parents. 小男孩接連不斷的問題終於惹火了他的爸媽。

❷ accede ▸ ac(to) + cede

v. 同意，就任，繼承

例：The man acceded to the heritage only to spent it over in only one month. 男子繼承財產，結果在一個月內就將其揮霍殆盡。

❸ antecedent ▸ ante（先前的 = before）+ ced + ent

adj. 先行的，前面的 n. 前例

例：With this antecedent, we should all be more careful when dealing with our clients. 有了此次先例，我們在面對客戶時都應更加謹慎。

❹ concede ▸ con（一起 = with）+ cede

v. 承認，讓步

例：The politician finally conceded that he bribed the voters.
該政客終於承認他賄賂選民。

❺ exceed ▸ ex(out) + ceed

v. 超越（限度），超過

例：You've exceed the speed limit. Haven't you noticed that?
你超速了。沒注意到嗎？

❻ recession ▸ re(back) + cess + ion

n.（經濟）衰退，後退

例：Economic recession is a global issue now.
經濟衰退現在已經是全球議題了。

❼ precede ▸ pre(before) + cede(go)

v. 領先，先行，佔優勢

例：The CEO precedes the head of the department, so you certainly listen to his opinions.
總裁高於部門主管，所以你當然應該聽他的意見。

❽ proceed ▸ pro（向前 = forward） + ceed

v. 著手繼續，開始，前進

例：After the shipping of the order, we proceed to the next one.
在此訂單產品出貨之後，我們進行下一筆。

❾ succeed ▸ suc(under) + ceed

v. 成功，繼承，隨……之後

例：We're all glad that we succeeded in winning the first prize.
成功拿到首獎，我們全部的人都很高興。

❿ accessory ▸ ac(to) + cess + ory

adj. 附加的，輔助的，同謀的 n. 配件，飾品，同謀

例：You don't need to wear too many accessories to this banquet.
參加此場宴會，你不需要配戴太多飾品。

Part 4 | 一般行為

clude、close 關

❶ closet ▸ clos + et（表示小的事物）

n. 碗櫥，衣櫥，小房間 adj. 私下的，秘密的

例：I hided in a closet in the attic during the hide-and-seek.
在玩捉迷藏的時候我躲在閣樓的一個小櫥櫃裡。

❷ disclose ▸ dis(not) + close

v. 打開，露出，使暴露，揭發

例：The reporter disclosed the secret information to the public.
該名記者向大眾揭發此項機密資訊。

❸ enclose ▸ en（使）+ close

v. 圍繞，包圍，封

例：The farmland is enclosed with wood fences. 木製籬笆圍住了農地。

❹ unclose ▸ un(not) + close

v. 打開

例：The window has remained unclosed for years since no one lives here. 因無人居住，窗戶多年未開。

❺ conclude ▸ con（一起 = with）+ clude

v. 達成結論，結束，推斷出

例：Please conclude your presentation with a concise summary.
請以簡短摘要結束你的報告。

❻ exclude ▸ ex(out) + clude

v. 把……除外，排除

例：Why did you exclude John from the class reunion?
你為何不讓約翰參與班聚？

❼ include ▸ in(into) + clude

v. 包含，含有

例：The set includes a serving of spaghetti, a side dish, and tomato soup.
此套餐包含一份義大利麵、配餐，以及番茄湯。

❽ preclude ▸ pre（先前的 = before） + clude

v. 防止，阻止，妨礙

例：We should preclude all potential malfunctions so we can get a satisfactory result.
要得到令人滿意的結果，我們應事先排除可能故障。

❾ seclude ▸ se(part) + clude

v. 分離，隔離，孤立，隱居

例：He secluded himself from the society and lived in a small town.
他遠離社會，居住在小鎮裡。

Part 4｜一般行為

clam、claim 喊

❶ claim ▶ 表示「喊，主張」的意思

v. 聲稱，要求，索賠 n. 要求，主張

例：The politician claimed that he was wronged by the allegation.
政客聲稱他遭受誣告。

❷ clamor ▶ clam + or

n. 大聲叫喊，喧嘩，喧鬧 v. 喊，喊

例：The clamor of the demonstration annoyed me.
遊行所發出的喧譁聲讓我不耐。

❸ disclaim ▶ dis(away) + claim

v. 放棄，否認

例：I officially disclaimed my right to succeed to the estate.
我正式放棄繼承財產。

❹ exclaim ▶ ex(out) + claim

v. 喊，驚呼

例：“Watch out for the car!” the mother exclaimed.
「小心車子！」媽媽驚呼。

❺ proclaim ▶ pro（向前 = forth） + claim

v. 公佈，宣告

例：The door was unclosed, proclaiming that someone was in the house. 門是開的，代表有人在房裡。

Part 4｜一般行為

cre、cru、crease 成長

❶ create ▸ cre + ate（動詞字尾）

v. 創造，創作

例：We together created a graffiti banner to show our support to the medical team.
我們共同創作了一幅塗鴉旗幟以示我們對醫療團隊的支持。

❷ decrease ▸ de(down) + crease

v. 減少，衰退 n. 減少（量）

例：Sales are decreasing due to the outbreak of the disease.
因疫情爆發，銷量減少了。

❸ increase ▸ in + crease

v./n. 增加，增長

例：We hope to increase our monthly budget for better product development.
為求更好的產品研發，我們希望可以增加每月預算。

❹ accretion ▸ ac(toward) + cre + tion

n. 增長（物），增加，堆積

例：The running of the new metro system leads to the accretion of population. 新捷運系統的營運增加了人口數量。

❺ recruit ▸ re + cruit

v. 招募 n. 新兵，新加入成員

例：The new recruits are said to be incompetent and need more training. 新來的成員據說能力不足，需要加強訓練。

cruc、crux 交叉

❶ crucial ▸ cruc + ial

adj. 關鍵的，至關重要的，重大的

例：Maintaining a work-life balance is crucial to one's quality of life.
維持生活和工作平衡對一個人的生活品質來說至關重要。

❷ crucify ▸ cruc + ify（動詞字尾）

v. 釘在十字架上處死，迫害，克制

例：Jesus Christ was said to be crucified on a crucifix.
耶穌基督據傳被釘在十字架上處死。

❸ crucifix ▸ cruc + i + fix（固定）

n. 十字架

例：The priest took out a crucifix and began the prayer.
牧師拿出十字架，開始禱告。

❹ cruciferous ▸ cruc + i + fer（攜帶 = carry） + ous

adj. 十字花科的，有十字形的

例：Cruciferous vegetables are commonly-used ingredients in Asian cuisine. 十字花科植物在亞洲料理中是常用的食材。

❺ excruciate ▸ ex(out) + cruci + ate

v. 使苦惱，施苦刑於

例：This excruciating pain made me sleepless at night.
這令人揪心的痛苦讓我夜晚失眠。

Part 4｜一般行為

cult 耕種

❶ cultivate ▸ cult + iv(e) + ate

v. 耕作，栽培，培育

例：Reading literature can actually cultivate your in-depth perspective toward the world. 閱讀文學其實可以培養對世界的深入觀點。

❷ culture ▸ cult + ure

n. 文化，培養，栽培

例：In western culture, people don't wear masks unless they are seriously ill. 在西方文化中，除非生重病，否則人們不會戴口罩。

❸ agriculture ▸ agri（農地 = soil） + culture

n. 農業

例：Agriculture accounts for a large percentage of GDP in Taiwan. 農業佔台灣 GDP 很高的比例。

❹ floriculture ▸ flori（花 = flower） + culture

n. 花卉栽培

例：My brother, after receiving his doctor's degree, decided to moved back home and focus on floriculture.
我哥哥在拿到博士學位之後，決定回鄉，專心進行花卉栽培。

❺ horticulture ▸ horti（花園） + culture

n. 園藝

例：Horticulture involves high technical skills and the sense of aesthetics. 園藝需要高超技藝和美感。

Part 4｜一般行為

cred、creed 信任

❶ creed ▶ 從「信任」延伸出

n. 信條，教義

例：No lying was my parent's creed in home education.
不說謊是我爸媽在家庭教育中的信念。

❷ credit ▶ cred + it(go)

n. 信用，貸款，功勞，學分，存款，（記帳）貸方 v. 信任，相信

例：I can't believe he took all the credit from the project.
我不敢相信他奪走了這個專案所有的功勞。

❸ credence ▶ cred + ence（名詞字尾）

n. 信用，憑證

例：We shouldn't give credence to gossips and rumors.
我們不應相信八卦和流言。

❹ credential ▶ cred + ent + ial

n. 信用證明，信任狀 adj. 信任的，可信賴的

例：I hope I can establish my credential as a resourceful field researcher.
我希望我能被證明具有作為一名學識豐富田野調查員的資格。

⑤ credible ▶ cred + ible（可以的）

adj. 可相信的，可靠的

例：This report is not credible at all. Don't believe it.
這篇報導完全不可信。別採信。

⑥ credulous ▶ cred + ul + ous

adj. 輕信的，易受騙的

例：The repetitive happenings of online scams root partly from credulous citizens.
層出不窮的網路詐騙案部分也是起因於人民易受騙。

⑦ incredible ▶ in（表否定）+ credible

adj. 無法相信的，無法信賴的，絕佳的

例：This performance is incredible! We should see it again!
這個表演太棒了！我們應該要再看一次！

⑧ accredit ▶ ac(to) + credit

v. 歸因於，委託，認可

例：The success of the disease control should be accredited to all who conform to the regulations.
疫情控制成功應被歸功於所有遵守規定的人。

⑨ discredit ▶ dis（遠離 = away）+ credit

v. 降低信用，敗壞名聲 n. 喪失名譽

例：The scandal has discredited himself as a professional negotiator.
這件醜聞已降低了他作為一名專業談判者的信用。

Part 4 | 一般行為

cur、cour 跑

❶ discourse ▸ dis(away) + course

n. 演講，論述 **v.** 談話，演講

例：The discourse was spot on and stroke a chord with the listeners.
這場演講精準到位，引起聽眾的共鳴。

❷ currency ▸ curr + ency

n. 通貨，流通，流傳，貨幣

例：Both Japanese Yen and US dollars are strong currencies.
日元和美元都是強勁貨幣。

❸ cursive ▸ curs + ive

adj. 草書的，草書體的 **n.** 草書

例：My professors tend to write in cursive when correcting our papers.
在修改我們的報告時，我的教授們喜歡以草書做書寫。

❹ extracurricular ▸ extra（額外的）+ curr + i + cular

adj. 課外的

例：Kids usually enjoy extracurricular activities such as playing dodgeball. 小孩通常喜歡課外活動，像是打躲避球。

❺ concur ▸ con（一起 = with） + cur

v. 同時發生，同意，一致，合作

例：Who could have predicted that these two events might concur and lead to deaths? 誰能夠預期到這兩起事件會同時發生並造成死亡？

❻ excursion ▸ ex(out) + curs + ion（名詞字尾）

n. 短途旅行，遠足，離題 v. 去郊遊

例：The excursion was cancelled due to the outbreak of the disease.
因疫情爆發，遠足被取消了。

❼ incur ▸ in(into) + cur

v. 招致，引起

例：Poor management of one's credit card use may incur debts.
信用卡使用的不當管理可能會帶來債務。

❽ occur ▸ oc(to) + cur

v. （事情等）發生，出現

例：During one's life, various events may occur, and that's how we become more mature.
在一個人的一生中，許多事情會發生，而這就是為什麼我們會變得更成熟。

❾ precursor ▸ pre（先前的 = before）+ curs + or（表事物）

n. 先驅，先鋒，前輩，前兆

例：Mr. Huang is hailed as the precursor of solar power development.
黃先生被譽為太陽能發展的先鋒。

❿ recur ▸ re(again) + cur(run)

v. 再次發生，復發

例：If you want the symptoms to stop recurring, take your medicine on time.
如果你希望症狀停止復發，就準時吃藥。

dic、dict 說

❶ dictate ▸ dict + ate

v. 聽寫，口述，命令，指示

例：The manager asked his secretary to dictate the CEO's speech.
經理要求其秘書聽寫紀錄總裁的演講。

❷ dictator ▸ dict + at(e) + or（表示人的字尾）

n. 獨裁者

例：All dictators, in any forms, should be overthrown.
以任何形式存在的獨裁者都應該被推翻。

❸ benediction ▸ bene（好的 = good）+ dict + ion

n. 祝福，恩賜，（飯前、飯後）感謝祈禱，（禮拜結束時的）祝禱

例：The priest began the benediction when everyone was seated.
在所有人坐定位之後，牧師開始祝禱。

❹ indicate ▸ in（裡面）+ dic + ate

v. 指示，表示

例：The announcement indicated that anyone failing to stay at home during the quarantine will be fined heavily.
公告表示，任何在隔離期間離開家的人都會被重罰。

❺ contradict ▸ contra(against) + dict

v. 矛盾，反駁，牴觸

例：Your words contradicted your actions. 你言行不一。

⑥ dedicate ▸ de(down) + dic + ate

v. 奉獻，致力於

例：I dedicated my whole life researching the relations of social economic structures and civil revolutions.
我花了一輩子的時間研究社經架構和公民革命之間的關係。

⑦ edict ▸ e(out) + dict

n. 佈告，法令，命令

例：The edict has met with severe public opinions.
新的法令遭受嚴重的社會輿論批評。

⑧ predict ▸ pre(before) + dict

v. 預言，預測

例：The control center predicted that the disease will continue to affect millions of people.
控制中心預測，此疾病會持續影響數百萬的人民。

⑨ verdict ▸ ver（真實 = truth）+ dict

n. 判決，裁定

例：The jury arrived at the verdict of guilty.
陪審團達成有罪的裁定。

⑩ jurisdiction ▸ juris（法律 = law）+ dict + ion

n. 司法權，裁判，支配權，管轄權

例：The council has no jurisdiction over any officials unaffiliated to it.
議會對不隸屬其單位的公務員不具管轄權。

Part 4｜一般行為

dyn 力量

❶ dynamics ▸ dynam + ics（科學）

n. 動力學，力學，動力

例：The dynamics of the overall economy in this country is still escalating. 這個國家的整體經濟動能仍持續上升。

❷ dynamite ▸ dynam + ite（表事物）

n. 炸藥 v. 炸毀

例：The army dynamited the bridge and ambushed the village.
軍隊用炸藥炸掉橋並埋伏村莊。

❸ dynasty ▸ dyn + ast（人）+ y

n. 王朝，朝代

例：The Tang dynasty was recorded to be filled with economic and cultural dynamics. 唐朝被記載為是充滿經濟和文化動力的朝代。

❹ aerodynamics ▸ aero（空氣 = air）+ dynamics

n. 空氣動力學

例：Aerodynamics is an elective course, so it depends on you whether to enroll in it or not.
空氣動力學是選修課，可以看你想不想要上這堂課。

❺ dynamic ▸ dynam + ic（表示有關的）

adj. 有活力的，力學的，動力學的

例：She is always so dynamic, easy-going, and open-minded.
她總是充滿活力、好相處，以及開明。

Part 4｜一般行為

duct、duce 引導

❶ abduct ▸ ab（遠離 = away） + duct

v. 誘拐，綁架

例：The heartless man abducted teenagers and asked for high ransoms. 這名無情的男子綁架青少年並要求高額贖金。

❷ conduce ▸ con（一起 = with） + duce

v. 導致（某種結果）（+ to），有益於，有貢獻於

例：Collaborations between citizens and the government turned out to conduce to cultural preservations.
公民和政府的合作證實有益於文化保存。

❸ conduct ▸ con（一起 = with） + duct

v. 表現，引導，指揮，傳導（熱、電等） n. 行為，執行，指導，指揮

例：Decent conducts determine one's prestige and reputation.
正直的行為決定了一個的聲望和名譽。

❹ deduce ▸ de(down) + duce

v. 推導（結論等），演繹，推論

例：We can deduce a reasonable theory on economic growth from this statistics. 我們可以從此統計數據中推理出對於經濟成長的合理理論。

❺ deduct ▸ de(down) + duct

v. 扣除

例：Remember to deduct unpaid payment from our profits.
記得要將未付貨款從收益中扣除。

❻ induce ▶ in(into) + duce

v. 引誘，誘發，導致

例：My long-term insomnia was induced by work pressure.
我的長期失眠是因工作壓力所導致。

❼ introduce ▶ intro(inward) + duce

v. 介紹，引導

例：May I introduce my parents to you? 我可以將我的家人介紹給你嗎？

❽ produce ▶ pro（向前的 = forth） + duce

v. 生產，製造，產生，製作 n. 農產品，產品

例：The play was first produced in the 80s, but remained mostly unnoticed until now.
這齣戲早在八零年代就首次演出，直到現在才受到矚目。

❾ reduce ▶ re（往回 = back） + duce

v. 減少，縮小，降低

例：I think we should reduce the scale of production now that sales are declining. 既然銷售量減少，我想我們應該縮減生產的規模。

❿ seduce ▶ se（遠離 = apart） + duce

v. 誘使，勾引，誘惑

例：My mom tried to seduce my sister to finish the meal with yummy snacks. 我媽媽試圖用美味的點心引誘我妹妹吃完食物。

fix 固定

❶ fixate ▸ fix + ate

v. 使固定，固定

例：My dad used a screwdriver to fixate the wood on the wall.
我爸爸用螺絲起子將木頭固定在牆上。

❷ affix ▸ af(to) + fix

v. 附加，貼上 n. 附加物，文綴

例：Please affix the file to the document and send it to us by noon.
請將文件附在檔案中並在中午前寄給我們。

❸ prefix ▸ pre（之前的 = before） + fix

n. 字首 v. 在……前加上

例：Learning prefixes can help you quickly determine the attribute when coming across a new word.
學習字首可以幫助你在遇到新的單字時快速決定其屬性。

❹ suffix ▸ suf（下面 = under） + fix

n. 字尾 v. 添加字尾

例：Suffixes usually indicate the location where they should be put in a sentence. 字尾通常表示其在一個句子中所屬的位置。

❺ transfix ▸ trans（穿透 = through） + fix

v. 刺穿，穿透，使動彈不得

例：The zombie was transfixed by a large spike and dropped dead instantly. 殭屍被一隻大釘刺穿，立即死亡。

flex、flect 彎曲

❶ flexible ▸ flex + ible（可以的）

adj. 易彎曲的，柔韌的，靈活的

例：Plastics are usually flexible and do not rust.
塑膠通常都是可以凹折且不會生鏽的。

❷ inflection ▸ in(into) + flect + ion

n. 彎曲，音調變化

例：The actor read the lines without inflection and bored the audience.
男演員毫無抑揚頓挫地念著台詞，讓觀眾覺得無趣。

❸ reflect ▸ re（再次 = again） + flect

v. 反射，反映，深思熟慮

例：I spend about ten minutes reflecting on what I have done at the end of the day. 我在一天結束前會花大概十分鐘的時間思考我做了什麼。

❹ deflection ▸ de(down) + flect + ion

n. 偏移，偏差，偏度

例：From this graph, we can observe the deflection of the arrow by the wind. 從這張圖表來看，我們可以觀察弓箭因風所產生的偏移。

❺ inflexible ▸ in(not) + flexible

adj. 不可彎曲的，不屈的，頑固的

例：Beware that the new regulation is inflexible and permanent.
請注意新規定是不受更改且長期有效的。

Part 4 | 一般行為

fac、fect、fic 製作

❶ factory ▸ fact + ory（表示地方）

n. 工廠

例：Both of my parents work in a manufacture factory nearby.
我爸媽都在附近的一間製造工廠工作。

❷ manufacture ▸ manu（手 = hand）+ fact + ure

n. 製造，製造業 v. 製造，生產

例：The factory where my parents work at mostly manufacture silk scarves. 我爸媽工作的工廠主要生產絲巾。

❸ affect ▸ af(to) + fect

v. 影響 n. 情感，感情

例：Aren't you aware that your behavior may affect the morale?
你難道沒有意識到你的行為會影響到士氣嗎？

❹ defect ▸ de(down) + fect

n. 缺點，弱點，不足，瑕疵 v. 逃跑，叛逃

例：Lack of efficiency is the major defect of this machine.
效能不彰是這台機器主要的缺點。

❺ effect ▸ ef（向外 = out）+ fect

n. 結果，效果，效力，影響 v. 產生（結果、效果），引起，實行

例：I don't think downsizing will produce any positive effect to the overall productivity. 我不認為縮編會對整體生產力有任何正面影響。

❻ perfect ▸ per（完全地 = completely）+ fect

adj. 完美的，精通的 v. 使完美

例：For my dad, my mom is perfect and he doesn't want to marry anyone else.
對我爸爸來説，我媽是完美的人，他不想娶其他人。

❼ fiction ▸ fict + ion（名詞字尾）

n. 虛構，小說，假像

例：Some claimed that reading fiction can magnify one's imagination.
有些人聲稱，讀虛構小說可以增強一個人的想像力。

❽ artificial ▸ arti（技能 = skill）+ fic + ial

adj. 人為的，人造的，不自然的，假裝的 n. 人造肥料

例：Artificial intelligence is the trend for mankind's future now.
人工智慧現在是人類未來的趨勢。

❾ deficient ▸ de（分離 = away）+ fic + ient

adj. 不足的，不充分的，缺乏的

例：Such theory is deficient in logical reasoning and analysis.
這個理論缺乏邏輯推論和分析。

❿ proficient ▸ pro（之前 = before）+ fic + ient

adj. 熟練的，嫻熟的

例：By the way he is looking so proficient in operating the machine, I bet he has been working here for a long time.
從他操作機器如此熟稔的方式來看，我猜他已經在這裡工作很久了。

forc、fort 強力的

❶ force ▶ 強的事物，力量

n. 力量，軍隊 v. 強迫

例：We should avoid the use of force during the demonstration.
在遊行中我們應避免使用暴力。

❷ enforce ▶ en（使）+ force

v. 強制，強加，實施

例：The government should enforce this law as soon as possible to prevent similar incidents from happening.
政府應盡快實施此項法律，以防類似事件再度發生。

❸ forte ▶ fort + e

n. 長處，特長 adj.（音樂）強音的

例：Math and chemistry are certainly not my forte.
數學和化學絕對不是我所擅長的。

❹ fortify ▶ fort + ify（動詞字尾）

v. 加強防禦，增強

例：During the war, the village was fortified with high stone walls.
在戰爭中，這座村莊建築高石牆以加強防禦。

❺ fortitude ▶ fort + itude（名詞字尾）

n. 不屈的精神，堅忍

例：My dad weathered through the storm with great fortitude.
我爸爸以堅忍不屈的精神度過了難關。

❻ effort ▸ ef（往外 = out）+ fort

n. 努力，費力，試圖

例：If you spare no efforts to finish the thesis, you are doomed to fail.
如果你不努力完成論文，你注定會失敗。

❼ comfort ▸ com（一起 = with）+ fort

n. 安慰，舒適

例：Many people seek comfort by buying lots of high-end products.
許多人透過購買高檔產品來尋求慰藉。

❽ discomfort ▸ dis(not) + comfort（舒適）

n. 不適，不舒服 v. 使不舒服

例：The discomforts of camping deterred me from joining any overnight trips in the mountain.
露營的不舒適讓我不想參加任何需要在山上過夜的旅程。

❾ uncomfortable ▸ un(not) + comfort + able

adj. 令人不舒服的，不自在的

例：Your rude words made me really uncomfortable and I think we should stop here.
你無禮的話讓我非常不舒服，我覺得我們談到這裡就好。

Part 4｜一般行為

fract、frag 破裂

❶ fracture ▸ fract + ure

n. 骨折，破裂，裂痕 v. 骨折，破裂，打破

例：The fracture of his leg is severe. 他的腿部骨折情況很嚴重。

❷ fragment ▸ frag(break) + ment → 破碎

n. 碎片（=part broken off），片段，分段 v. 破裂

例：My dad fell from a ladder and fractured both of his legs.
我爸爸從梯架上跌了下來，兩隻手臂都骨折了。

❸ fragile ▸ frag + ile（可以的）

adj. 易碎的，脆弱的

例：The vase is very fragile. Please be careful during shipping.
這個花瓶非常易碎。運送時請小心一點。

❹ infraction ▸ in + fract + ion

n. 違反，違背，違法

例：The infraction of civil laws may involve a large amount of compensation. 違反民法可能會牽涉大筆賠償金。

❺ refraction ▸ re（再次 = again）+ fract + ion

n.（光、聲音、熱等）折射

例：Our teacher asked us to observe the refraction by turning on the projector. 我們老師要我們打開投影機，觀察光的折射。

fer 攜帶

❶ ferry ▸ fer + ry

n. 渡口（碼頭），擺渡（船）*v.* 擺渡，用船運送

例：The cargo was transported to the ferry, waiting to be further assigned. 貨品被送至渡口，等待進一步分派。

❷ confer ▸ con（一起 = with）+ fer

v. 協商，授予

例：The diploma was finally conferred on me, meaning that I passed the oral presentation. 我終於被授予文憑，代表我通過口試了。

❸ differ ▸ dif（分開 = away）+ fer

v. 不同，意見不同，差異

例：When my opinion differs with my partner's, we usually agree to disagree. 當我的想法和我的另一半不同時，我們通常會尊重對方意見。

❹ infer ▸ in（之中）+ fer

v. 推論，得出結論，推測

例：From this piece of article, we can infer that global warming is only getting worse. 從這篇文章中我們可以得知，全球暖化越趨嚴重。

❺ offer ▸ of（朝向 = toward）+ fer

v. 提供，提案，提議 *n.* 提供，提案，求婚，意圖，開價

例：I'm afraid that we can't accept this offer. The price is too high.
恐怕我們無法接受此開價。價格太高了。

❻ prefer ▸ pre（之前 = before）+ fer

v. 偏好，較喜歡

例：I prefer wearing jeans to skirts since I run on the street a lot!
我喜歡穿牛仔褲勝過裙子，因為我很常在街上奔跑！

❼ refer ▸ re(back, again) + fer

v. 歸因於，提到，參考，提交

例：During the course, the professor frequently referred to Jane Austen's works.
在這堂課中，教授時常提及珍奧斯丁的作品。

❽ suffer ▸ suf（之下 = under）+ fer

v. 受苦，經歷，忍受

例：I've been suffering from insomnia for years and it's killing me.
我飽受失眠之苦已經好幾年了，痛不欲生。

❾ transfer ▸ trans（橫越 = across）+ fer

v. 轉移，轉讓（財產等） **n.** 轉移，換乘，轉讓

例：Remember to transfer the money to Adam in time. We promised him.
記得要即時轉錢給亞當，我們答應過他了。

❿ defer ▸ de(down) + fer

v. 推遲，延期

例：It's good that many people decided to defer their trip due to the outbreak of the disease.
許多人因為疫情爆發決定延遲旅行，這是好消息。

fin 限制、界線

❶ final ▸ fin + al

adj. 最終的，最後的，不可更改的

例：The verdict is final. All appeals should be denied.
此為最終判決。拒絕所有上訴。

❷ finesse ▸ fin + esse

n. 技巧，計謀，策略，手腕 v. 施展巧計，使用策略

例：The negotiator closed the deal with great finesse.
談判官以高超手腕談成交易。

❸ finish ▸ fin + ish

v. 結束，完成

例：My mother asked my brother to finish the meal before7 o'clock.
我媽媽要求我弟弟在七點前吃完飯。

❹ confine ▸ con（一起 = together）+ fine

v. 禁閉，監禁，使臥床 n. 邊界，界線

例：My father was confined to bed by a serious illness for weeks.
我爸爸因重病臥床好幾個禮拜。

❺ define ▸ de(down) + fine

v. 下定義

例：Define "freedom" before you talk about the search for freedom.
在談論對於自由的追求之前，請先定義「自由」。

❻ infinite ▸ in（表否定）+ fin + ite

adj. 無限的，無數的

例：There are an infinite number of stars shining in the sky.
天上有無數的星星在閃爍。

❼ refine ▸ re（再次= again）+ fine

v. 精煉，提煉，雕琢

例：Reading and writing are sure to refine your word choices.
閱讀和寫作絕對能雕琢你的用字。

❽ definite ▸ de(down) + fin + ite

adj. 明確的，精確的，確實的

例：We need a definite figure to estimate the budget for next year.
我們需要準確的數據來預測明年的預算。

❾ affinity ▸ af（近的= near）+ fin + ity

n. 姻親（關係），近似，傾向

例：Taiwanese orchids have a close affinity to those in Japan.
台灣蘭花和日本蘭花很類似。

Part 4｜一般行為

grac、grat 快樂、感激

❶ gracious ▶ grac + ious（形容詞字尾）

adj.（人品、態度）親切的，慈祥的

例：My grandparents are always gracious to anyone paying a visit.
我的爺爺奶奶對任何拜訪他們的人都很親切。

❷ disgrace ▶ dis（偏離 = away）+ grace

n. 恥辱，丟臉 v. 使丟臉

例：You are such a disgrace to the family! 你真是這個家庭的恥辱！

❸ grateful ▶ grate + ful（形容詞字尾）

adj. 感謝的，表示謝意的

例：I will be forever grateful to your kind help.
對你的善意幫忙，我會永存感激。

❹ gratitude ▶ grat + itude（狀態）

n. 感謝，謝意，感激

例：She showed great gratitude to her parents in the graduation speech. 在畢業致詞中，她表達了對父母的巨大感激。

❺ ingratitude ▶ in（表否定）+ grat + itude

n. 忘恩負義

例：His ingratitude disappointed his sponsors, so they cancelled all financial support.
他的忘恩負義讓他的贊助商們感到失望，因此決定取消對他的金援。

grav 重的

❶ grave ▶ 重的事物

adj. 重大的，嚴肅的 n. 墳墓

例：The grave tone of her speech made everyone sentimental.
她演說的嚴肅音調讓所有人多愁善感。

❷ gravitate ▶ grav + it(go) + ate

v. 受引力作用，被吸引

例：The attention of the guests gravitated toward the door when the host came in. 當主人進門時，賓客們的注意力都轉向門邊。

❸ aggravate ▶ ag（朝向= to） + grav + ate

v. 加劇，使惡化

例：The illness aggravated through time, and we weren't hopeful.
病情隨著時間過去逐漸惡化，而且我們也不抱希望。

❹ engrave ▶ en（使） + grave

v. 雕刻，銘記

例：I want to engrave my parents' names on this timepiece.
我想在這個鐘上刻上我父母親的名字。

❺ gravity ▶ grav + ity（名詞字尾）

n. 重力，嚴重性，重大，嚴肅

例：By gravity, the rocks fell and scattered all over the floor.
石頭因為重力掉了下來，散落在地上。

greg 群體

❶ gregarious ▸ greg + arious（形容詞字尾）

adj. 群居的，好社交的

例：My sister is such a gregarious person that she goes out every night. 我姊姊是個愛交際的人，每天晚上都出門。

❷ aggregate ▸ ag（朝向= to）+ greg + ate

v. 聚集 n. 集合，聚集，總數 adj. 總計的

例：The aggregate number of the audience is 5 thousands.
總計觀眾共有五千人。

❸ congregate ▸ con（一起= with）+ greg + ate

n. 聚集，集合，成團

例：The protestors congregated in front of the park for the sit-in.
抗議人士聚集在公園前面準備靜坐。

❹ egregious ▸ e（向外= out）+ greg + ious

adj. 極為惡劣的，非常的，令人震驚的

例：Such egregious delinquency should be heavily puninshed.
如此惡劣的違法行徑應該被嚴懲。

❺ segregate ▸ se（分離= apart）+ greg + ate

n. 分離，隔離

例：The government segregated the demonstrators and confined them against the law. 政府隔離遊行人士，並非法將他們監禁起來。

Part 4｜一般行為

flu 流動

❶ fluent ▶ flu + ent（具某種性質的）

adj. 流暢的，流利的，流動的

例：Her English is really fluent, so I study very hard to catch up with her. 她的英文非常流利，所以我努力學習想要跟上她。

❷ fluid ▶ flu + id（表某種狀態的）

adj. 流動性的，流動的，易變的 n. 流體

例：Her fluid writing style won her instant academic appraisal.
她流暢的寫作風格讓她立即獲得學術界的讚賞。

❸ flux ▶ flu + x

n. 流動，流出，漲潮

例：Economic growth is always in a state of flux.
經濟成長總是處於不停的變化狀態。

❹ fluctuate ▶ fluct + u + ate

v. 波動，動搖，變動

例：The fluctuating numbers on the screen make all the investors nervous. 螢幕上不斷變動的數字讓所有投資者感到緊張。

❺ affluent ▶ af（朝向=to）+ flu + ent

adj. 富裕的，豐富的，富足的

例：This region is rather affluent; people here drive fancy cars and carry high-end bags.
這個區域住很多有錢人。這裡的人都開跑車和背高檔包包。

❻ influence ▸ in(into) + flu + ence（名詞字尾）

n. 影響

例：Don't you know that your behavior has a great influence on your siblings?
你不知道你的行為對你的兄弟姐妹造成很大的影響嗎？

❼ influenza ▸ in(into) + flu + enza

n. 流行性疾病

例：The influenza added hail to snow when the country is already suffering from depression.
此流行性疾病對這個經濟正在衰退中的國家來說簡直是雪上加霜。

❽ confluence ▸ con（一起= together）+ flu + ence

n. 匯集，匯流

例：We gathered at the confluence of the two rivers to appreciate the waterfall.
我們站在這兩條河的匯流處欣賞瀑布。

❾ fluency ▸ flu + ency（名詞字尾）

n. 流利，流暢度

例：Fluency in both Chinese and English is prerequisite for this position.
中英流利是此職位的必備條件。

Part 4｜一般行為

lev 輕的、上升

❶ levity ▸ lev + ity（名詞字尾）

n. 多變，輕率，不穩定，輕浮

例：This banquet is not for levity, so behave yourself.
這宴會是非常正經的，所以請注意你的言行。

❷ levitate ▸ lev + it(go) + ate

v. 使漂浮空中，使漂浮

例：The trick was about levitating coins and align them in the air.
這個把戲是將硬幣漂浮於空中，並將它們排成一直線。

❸ alleviate ▸ al（朝向= to）+ levi + ate

v. 減輕，緩和

例：The pain finally alleviated, but the sore remained.
痛苦終於減緩了，但是痠感還是存在。

❹ elevate ▸ e（向外= out）+ lev + ate

v. 提升，提高，提拔

例：We all need to elevate ourselves through reading, writing, and constant reflections.
我們都需要透過閱讀、寫作，以及不斷地自省來提升自己。

❺ leverage ▸ lev + er + age（集合名詞字尾）

n. 抗橫手段，槓桿 v. 起槓桿作用

例：His professional negotiation skills is giving the team leverage on the deal. 他專業的協商技巧在交易上起了很大的作用。

liber、liver 自由

❶ liberal ▸ liber + al（形容次字尾）

adj. 心胸寬大的，自由主義的，大方的，大量的 n. 自由主義者

例：My dad is surprisingly very liberal to tattoos.
我爸爸令人意外地對於刺青抱持開放態度。

❷ liberate ▸ liber + ate（動詞字尾）

v. 解放，釋放

例：I hope one day, all of us can be liberated from capitalism and understand the meaning of true freedom.
我希望有天，我們都能從資本主義中解放，並明白真正自由的意義。

❸ liberty ▸ liber + ty（名詞字尾）

n. 自由，解放，許可

例：May I take the liberty to request the number of the sales?
我可以冒昧詢問你銷售數據嗎？

❹ deliver ▸ de(down) + liver

v. 交付，遞送，發表

例：My mother is going to deliver an important speech she's been preparing for weeks.
我媽媽準備要發表一場她準備了好幾個禮拜的重要演說。

❺ libertine ▸ liber + tine（之人）

n. 浪蕩子，玩樂者

例：He is quite a modern libertine, spending all the time and money on entertainment.
他真是現代版的浪子，將所有時間和金錢花在娛樂上。

Part 4 | 一般行為

grad、gress 步伐

❶ graduate ▸ grad + u + ate

v. 畢業，分等級

例：I finally graduated from the program after three years of hard work.
經過三年的努力，我終於從這個課程中畢業了。

❷ gradual ▸ grad + ual（表性質）

adj. 逐步的，逐漸的

例：Even though the progress is gradual, you are still improving.
雖然過程很緩慢，但你確實在進步當中。

❸ degrade ▸ de(down) + grade

v. 使降級，貶低

例：The man was degraded for forgery.
這個男人因為偽造罪降低了自己的人格。

❹ upgrade ▸ up(upward) + grade

v. 使升級，提升 n. 升級

例：You need to upgrade your anti-virus software.
你需要升級你的防毒軟體。

❺ congress ▸ con（一起= together）+ gress

n. 國會，議會（大寫首字母）

例：The Congress finally reached the consensus and passed the bill.
國會最終達成協議，通過法案。

❻ digress ▶ di（遠離= away）+ gress

v. 走向岔道，離題

例：To digress for a moment, what are we having for lunch?
離題一下，我們午餐要吃什麼？

❼ progress ▶ pro（向前的= forward）+ gress

n. 前進，發展，進步 v. 進步，前進，進行

例：Even though I'm making progress, it doesn't show on my grades.
儘管我有進步，但成績仍無起色。

❽ transgress ▶ trans（橫越= across）+ gress

v. 違反（法律等），侵犯，越界

例：You've already transgress the lawful limits made by the government, and should hence be fined.
你已經違反了政府訂定的法律限制，所以應該被罰款。

❾ aggressive ▶ ag（朝向= to）+ gress + ive

adj. 攻擊的，積極的，好戰的

例：The enemy took an aggressive stance and launched attacks everyday. 敵方採取積極攻勢，每天發動攻擊。

❿ retrograde ▶ retro（倒退的= backward）+ grade

v. 倒退，退步，逆行 adj. 後退的，退化的

例：The retrograde motion of the ball indicated that the river flowed counterclockwise. 球向後方移動表示這條河是朝逆時針方向流動的。

Part 4｜一般行為

hum 土地

❶ humble ▸ hum + ble

adj. 謙遜的 v. 使謙恭

例：He is knowledgeable and prestigious, yet he is very humble.
他飽讀詩書且享負盛名，卻非常謙虛。

❷ humidity ▸ hum + id + ity（名詞字尾）

n. 濕氣，濕度

例：The high humidity in Taipei is the main reason why Imoved back home. 台北的高濕度是我搬回家的主要原因。

❸ humiliate ▸ hum + ili + ate

v. 使丟臉，羞辱，恥辱

例：Why did you say those words to humiliate me in front of the guests? 你為什麼要在賓客面前說那些話羞辱我？

❹ exhume ▸ ex（向外= out）+ hume

v. 掘出（屍體），發掘

例：Three bodies were exhumed on the hill in the remote mountain.
三具屍體從偏遠的山上被挖了出來。

❺ posthumous ▸ post（之後的）+ hum + ous

adj. 死後的，死後出版的

例：Sarcastically, many writers went famous through their posthumous works. 諷刺的是，許多作家是透過死後才出版的作品才成名。

ject 丟、投擲

❶ abject ▸ ab（遠離的= away）+ ject

adj. 可憐的，卑鄙的，不幸的

例：He remained his dignity even at the time of abject misery.
就連在悲慘困苦的時刻，他仍保有他的尊嚴。

❷ conjecture ▸ con（一起= with）+ ject + ure

n. 推測，猜想 v. 猜測，推測

例：His conjecture on economic growth was soon proved solid.
他對經濟發展的推測很快就被證實有用。

❸ deject ▸ de(down) + ject

v. 使灰心，使沮喪

例：The woman looked sorrowful and dejected. We wondered what happened to her.
女子看起來很哀傷且垂頭喪氣。我們在想她發生了什麼事。

❹ eject ▸ e（向外的=out）+ ject

v. 噴射，驅逐，逐出，彈出

例：Please press the “eject” button before you take out your USB from the computer. 在你將 USB 從電腦中取出時，請按「退出」按鈕。

❺ inject ▸ in(into) + ject

v. 注入，注射

例：The nurse injected glucose into my veins.
護士將葡萄糖注射至我的血管內。

❻ interject ▶ inter（之間= between）+ ject

v. 插嘴，突然插入

例：I considered him a rude man, for he frequently interjected his comments during the Q&A session.
我覺得他是個很無理的人，因為他在問答時間不斷地插入他的想法。

❼ object ▶ ob（反抗=against）+ ject

n. 物體，客體，目標，受詞 v. 反對，抗議

例：My object is to make everyone feel well-treated in thebanquet.
我的目標是讓所有人在宴會中備受款待。

❽ project ▶ pro（向前= forth）+ ject

n. 計畫，企劃，專案 v. 投射，放映，計畫

例：I was assigned three large-scale projects this month and no one helped me. 我這個月被分派三個大規模專案且沒有人幫我。

❾ reject ▶ re(back) + ject

v. 拒絕，丟棄，駁回 n. 被棄之人或物，被拒絕的人

例：The man's application for parole was rejected.
男子申請假釋，但被駁回。

❿ subject ▶ sub（之下= under）+ ject

n. 主題，科目，（文法）主詞 adj. 服從的，易患……的
v. 使服從，使隸屬於

例：My sister is subject to migraine and no medication can cure this symptom.
我姊姊常常偏頭痛，且吃什麼藥都不會好。

Part 4｜一般行為

join、junct 連接

❶ adjoin ▸ ad(to) + join

v. 鄰近，毗鄰

例：Taichung adjoins Changhua. 台中靠近彰化。

❷ disjoin ▸ dis（遠離= off）+ join

v. 使分開，分離

例：You need to disjoin these two bricks so that they can be placed at the right place.
你需要先將這兩個磚塊分開，才能後續將它們放置在正確的位置。

❸ injunct ▸ in（向內= into）+ junct

v. 下令禁止，命令

例：The government attempted to injunct further reports on this issue.
政府試圖下令禁止對該議題的進一步報導。

❹ conjunction ▸ con（一起= together）+ junct + ion

n. 連接，關聯，連接詞

例：You need conjunctions to link two separate sentences together.
你需要連接詞才能將兩個不同的句子連接在一起。

❺ adjunct ▸ ad（近的= near）+ junct

n. 附屬物，修飾語，助手 adj. 附屬的

例：My dad used to an adjunct professor at National Taiwan Normal University. 我爸曾是台灣師範大學的兼職教授。

Part 4 | 一般行為

migr 移動

❶ migrate ▸ migr + ate（動詞字尾）

v. 遷移，移動，遷徙

例：Birds usually migrate to the south during winters.
鳥類通常會在冬季遷徙至南方。

❷ emigrate ▸ e（向外的= out）+ migrate

v. 移居國外

例：My neighbors decided to emigrate to Taiwan due to the disease.
我的鄰居因疫情決定移居至台灣。

❸ immigrate ▸ im（向內的= into）+ migrate

v. 使移居入境，移入

例：It is said that my ancestors immigrated from Germany to Taiwan for better living environment.
據說我的祖先因為追求更好的生活環境從德國移居台灣。

❹ transmigrate ▸ trans（橫越= across）+ migrate

v. 移居，轉世

例：In this book, the author said that the souls of men transmigrated into animals or plants.
在這本書中，作者說人類的靈魂會轉世成動物或植物。

❺ migrant ▸ migr + ant

adj. 移居的 n. 移居者

例：Migrants suffered more than we think, so we should have sympathy for them.
移民遭受的痛苦比我們想得多，所以我們應該要對他們保有同情心。

Part 4｜一般行為

loc 地方

❶ local ▸ loc + al

adj. 當地的，地方性的，局部的

例：I always try to savor local cuisine when traveling.
在旅遊時，我總是試著品嚐當地美食。

❷ locate ▸ loc + ate

v. 查找……的地點，位於

例：The police failed to locate the crime scene right away, so the case took years to solve.
警方未能立即找出案發現場，所以花了好幾年的時間才破案。

❸ allocate ▸ al(to) + loc + ate

v. 分派，分配

例：The government should allocate daily supplies equally to the public. 政府應該要平均發放物資給大眾。

❹ dislocate ▸ dis（遠離=away）+ loc + ate

v. 使脱臼，使移位

例：My brother dislocated his arm when training for the track and field.
我弟弟在田徑訓練時手臂脱臼了。

❺ relocate ▸ re（再次= again）+ loc + ate

v. 重新安置，遷移

例：We need to relocate your father to another nursing home.
我們需要將你父親重新安置到另一個安養院。

Part 4｜一般行為

miss、mit 發送

❶ missile ▸ miss + ile

n. 飛彈 adj. 可發射的，導彈的

例：The enemy launched several nuclear missiles and the third world war began. 敵方發射幾枚核彈，第三次世界大戰自此展開。

❷ admit ▸ ad（朝向= to）+ mit

v. 允許，承認

例：I admitted that I made a mistake and my parents forgave me at last. 我承認犯錯，父母最後也原諒了我。

❸ commit ▸ com（共同= with）+ mit

v. 犯（罪或者錯誤），作出承諾，交付

例：I don't want to commit anything to you now.
我目前不想對你做出任何承諾。

❹ dismiss ▸ dis（偏離 = away）+ miss

v. 解散，解雇，使離開

例：The meeting was dismissed immediately after the earthquake.
在地震過後，會議即刻解散。

❺ emit ▸ e（向外= out）+ mit(send)

v. 散發（光、熱、氣味之類），發出，發表

例：The jewelry emitted an eery circle of light. 寶石發出詭異的光圈。

❻ intermittent ▸ inter（之間= between）+ mit + t + ent

adj. 間歇的，斷斷續續的，週期性的

例：The intermittent rain hindered us from going out for walk.
間歇雨讓我們無法外出散步。

❼ permit ▸ per（完全地= completely）+ mit

v. 允許，許可 n. 認可證，執照

例：The dean of the department didn't permit us to hold a demonstration on campus. 院長不允許我們在校內舉辦遊行。

❽ remit ▸ re（退回= back）+ mit

v. 匯款，緩和，減退，免除

例：The accountant asked us to remit the money by Friday.
會計師要求我們在週五前匯款。

❾ submit ▸ sub（之下= under）+ mit

v. 服從，臣服，提交

例：I submitted to her glamor and promised to be her friend forever.
我臣服於她的魅力之下，並承諾永遠當她的朋友。

❿ transmit ▸ trans（橫越=across）+ mit

v. 傳輸，傳播，發送

例：Find a way to make the machine transmit energy efficiently, okay?
找個方法讓機器可以有效輸能，好嗎？

Part 4 | 一般行為

mob、mov、mot 移動

❶ mobile ▶ mob + ile（可以的）

adj. 可移動的，活動的，流動的 n. 汽車

例：You can buy cheap second-hand books in that mobile library.
你可以在流動圖書館裡買到便宜的二手書。

❷ mobilize ▶ mob + il(e) + ize（動詞字尾）

v. 動員（軍隊之類），調動，集合

例：The government quickly mobilized the troops, ready to fight the war. 政府快速動員軍隊，準備迎戰。

❸ automobile ▶ auto（自我= self）+ mob + ile

n. 汽車 adj. 汽車的

例：Having an automobile actually involves a lot of extra costs.
擁有一台車實際上需要更多其他花費。

❹ motion ▶ mot + ion（名詞字尾）

n. 動作，移動

例：Why did that beautiful woman seem to move in a slow motion?
為什麼那名美麗的女子好像以慢動作在移動？

❺ motivate ▶ mot + iv(e) + ate

v. 賦予動機，刺激

例：My parents' love is what motivates me to get my master's degree.
我父母親的愛是激勵我完成碩士學位的動力。

❻ motor ▸ mot + or（事物）

n. 馬達，發動機，汽車

例：With a broken motor, we were stuck on the boat in the middle of the lake. 馬達壞掉了，我們被困在湖中央的船上。

❼ commotion ▸ com（一起= together）+ mot + ion

n. 騷動，暴動

例：The commotion last night really scared me and I didn't dare to go out this morning.
昨晚的騷動真的嚇到我了，我今天早上不敢出門。

❽ promote ▸ pro（向前= forward）+ mote

v. 提升，促進，升職

例：I finally got promoted after working extra hours for three months in a row. 在連續三個月加班之後，我終於升職了。

❾ remove ▸ re（向後 = back）+ move

v. 移動，遷移，開除 n. 移動

例：Could you kindly remove your car in front of the store?
可以麻煩你好心將你停在店前的車子移開嗎？

❿ emotion ▸ e(out) + motion

n. 情感，情緒

例：I felt a surge of emotions in me when I saw the painting.
看到那幅畫的時候，我情緒泉湧。

Part 4 | 一般行為

pend 懸掛

❶ pendulum ▶ pend + ul + um（表事物）

n. 鐘擺，搖錘

例：The pendulum hanging in the lobby was beautifully-designed.
懸掛在大廳的鐘擺設計得很漂亮。

❷ suspend ▶ sus（之下= under）+ pend

v. 使暫停，延緩，停學，停職，暫停營業

例：He was suspended when the professor found out that he copied online materials in his paper.
因為教授發現他的報告抄襲網路資料，他就被停學了。

❸ depend ▶ de(down) + pend

v. 依賴，依靠，取決於

例：I hope my loved ones can depend on me, be it financially or spiritually. 我希望無論是經濟上還是心靈上，我所愛的人都能依靠我。

❹ independence ▶ in（表否定）+ de + pend + ence

n. 獨立，自立性

例：Seeking independence is one of the goals for young people leaving home for work. 追求獨立是許多離家工作年輕人的目標之一。

❺ impending ▶ im（向內= into）+ pend + ing

adj. 迫近的，即將發生的

例：The impending final exam put a lot of pressure on the students.
即將到來的期末考讓學生備感壓力。

press 壓

❶ pressure ▸ press + ure

n. 壓力，壓迫，按壓 v. 壓、按、壓迫、催促

例：Working at home is still a lot of pressure, especially when there are many distractions.
在家工作仍然有很大的壓力，尤其有很多分心的事物。

❷ pressurize ▸ pressur + ize（動詞字尾）

v. 〔航空〕（高空飛行中氣密艙的）密封，增壓

例：Please send this liquid to the Pressurized Reaction Chamber.
請將此液體送至加壓反應室。

❸ compress ▸ com（一起 = together） + press

v. 壓縮，壓緊

例：These dried flowers can be compressed into the thin wood, and they will make beautiful bookmarks.
可以將這些乾燥花壓進薄木裡面，它們就會成為美麗的書籤。

❹ depress ▸ de(down) + press

v. 使沮喪消沈，壓低

例：The news depressed all of us, and we wish her a quick recovery.
這個消息讓我們所有人感到難過，希望她能快速康復。

⑤ express ▸ ex（向外的 = out）+ press

v. 表達，表示 n. 快遞，快車 adj. 快遞的，明確陳述的

例：I sometimes don't know how to express my feelings clearly.
有時候不知道該如何清楚地表達我的感受。

⑥ impress ▸ im（向內）+ press

v. 留下生動的印象，使感動，使銘記

例：Your oral presentation impressed all the interviewers.
你的口試報告讓所有面試官留下深刻印象。

⑦ oppress ▸ op（對抗 = against）+ press

v. 壓迫，壓抑

例：Should the government oppress the people, a revolution is soon to come. 如果政府壓迫人民，革命就不遠了。

⑧ repress ▸ re(back) + press

v. 抑制，壓迫，鎮壓

例：Try to repress your anger first, and find a way to communicate.
先抑制你的憤怒，然後找個辦法溝通。

⑨ suppress ▸ sup(under) + press

v. 鎮壓，壓制，抑制

例：It is because the government suppressed the news that the disease became a pandemic.
正是因為政府封鎖消息，這個疾病才會廣泛流行。

Part 4｜一般行為

pris 抓

❶ prison ▸ 抓住並放下的地方

n. 監獄 v. 監禁，關押

例：The murderer was finally sentenced and put into jail.
謀殺者終於被判刑入獄。

❷ comprise ▸ com（一起）+ prise

v. 包含，由……組成

例：The set is comprised of three earphones and three headsets.
這個套組包含三個耳機和三個頭戴式耳機。

❸ enterprise ▸ enter（之間= inter）+ prise

n. 事業，進取心，事業，企業

例：The spirit of enterprise is essential if you want to start your own business. 如果你想要創業的話，進取心很重要。

❹ imprison ▸ im（放入內= into）+ pris + on

v. 關押，監禁，使……入獄

例：The police imprisoned the serial killer after decades of investigation.
在幾十年的調查之後，警方將該名連續殺人犯關入獄。

❺ surprise ▸ sur（之上= over）+ prise

v. 使驚奇，使驚訝，使感到意外 n. 驚喜，驚奇

例：The present surprised me and I was moved to tears.
這個禮物出乎我意料，使我感動流淚。

priv 個人

❶ privacy ▸ priv + acy（名詞字尾）

n. 隱私，隱居，秘密

例：The actress is very protective of her family's privacy.
這位女明星非常保護她家人的隱私。

❷ privilege ▸ privi + leg（法律= law）+ e

n. 特權 v. 賦予……特權

例：The king granted the duke the privilege to access the secret chamber. 國王賦予公爵進入秘密房間的特權。

❸ deprive ▸ de(not) + prive

v. 剝奪，使喪失

例：Who are you to deprive me of the right of speech?
你有什麼資格剝奪我的言論自由？

❹ underprivileged ▸ under + privileged

adj. 貧困的，被剝奪基本權利的，社會地位低下的

例：I feel sorry for the underprivileged and hope they get what they deserve. 我對低層階級的人感到同情，並希望他們得到其所應得的。

❺ private ▸ priv + ate

adj. 私人的，私有的

例：This is a private property, open to VIPs only.
這是私人土地，僅開放給貴賓。

Part 4｜一般行為

port 運送

❶ portable ▶ port + able（可以的）

adj. 手提的，可攜式的 **n.** 手提式物品

例：The computer is portable and light; besides, it's really cheap.
這個電腦是手提的，而且很輕。除此之外，它很便宜。

---

❷ airport ▶ air + port

n. 機場

例：Most of the airports are not so busy now, especially international ones.
大多數的機場現今都沒有那麼繁忙了，尤其是國際機場。

---

❸ comport ▶ com（共同= together）+ port

v. 行為，舉動，合適，一致

例：This book will teach you how to comport yourself and win others over.
這本書會教你如何舉止得宜，贏得他人的喜歡。

---

❹ deport ▶ de(down) + port

v. 驅逐出境，舉止，放逐

例：The man was deported right after he was found carrying drugs at the airport.
男子因為在機場被發現攜帶毒品，立即遭到驅逐出境。

❺ export ▸ ex（向外= out）+ port

v. 出口 **n.** 出口物，出口額，出口業

例：Our company mainly export agricultural produce, sometimes hand-made soaps.
我們公司主要出口農產品，但有時也會出口手工香皂。

❻ import ▸ im（向內= into）+ port

v. 進口（商品），意義 **n.** 進口（貨）

例：We used to import masks, but now, we make our own.
我們過去是進口口罩，但現在，我們自己做。

❼ report ▸ re(again) + port

n.（調查，研究的）報告，報導，成績單 **v.** 報導，報告

例：Each of you has to report this issue from different perspectives.
你們每一個人都需要從不同的觀點報導此議題。

❽ support ▸ sup（之下= under）+ port

v. 支持，援助，支撐 **n.** 支援，支撐（物）

例：I cut off my financial support to my son to make him independent.
我斷絕對兒子的金援，幫助他獨立。

❾ transport ▸ trans（橫越= across）+ port

v. 運輸 **n.** 輸送，運送

例：We need to transport the products to Germany on time, or they'll cancel the order.
我們需要準時將商品運輸至德國，不然他們會取消訂單。

Part 4｜一般行為

pose 放置

❶ compose ▸ com（一起= together）+ pose

V. 由……構成，作曲，使平靜

例：This piece of symphony was composed by the famous Mozart.
這首交響曲是由知名的莫札特所作的。

❷ depose ▸ de(down) + pose

V. 免職，廢黜

例：The queen was deposed due to her misjudgment on economy.
皇后因對經濟誤判被罷黜了。

❸ dispose ▸ dis（遠離 = away）+ pose

V. 處理，配置

例：Make sure you dispose of these second-hand books before the warden came back. 在典獄長回來之前，你要將這些二手書處理好。

❹ expose ▸ ex(out) + pose

V. 揭露，揭發，使曝光

例：The reporter exposed the scandal and the president resigned.
該名記者揭露弊案，總統因而下台。

❺ impose ▸ im(into) + pose

V. 徵稅，強加負擔，欺騙

例：Why did the government impose such a heavy tax on cigarette?
為什麼政府要向菸徵收重稅？

❻ interpose ▶ inter（之間= between）+ pose

v. 插入，干預，調停，提出

例：I'd like to interpose an objection on the verdict.
我想要針對判決提出異議。

❼ oppose ▶ op(against) + pose

v. 反對，反抗

例：The new law is strongly opposed by the public, and I think the Congress should sleep on it.
新法案遭受大眾強力反對，我認為國會應該多加審視。

❽ propose ▶ pro（向前的 = forward）+ pose

v. 建議，計畫，求婚

例：Have you heard that Adam proposed to Lily yesterday?
你聽說亞當昨晚向莉莉求婚了嗎？

❾ purpose ▶ pur（完全地 = completely）+ pose

n. 目的，意志，用途

例：I didn't do it on purpose. It was a pure accident.
我不是故意的。這純屬意外。

❿ suppose ▶ sup（之下= under）+ pose

v. 假設，推測，認為

例：Let's suppose that you got the scholarship. What are you going to choose as your major?
我們先假設你拿到獎學金了。
那你要選什麼當主修？

Part 4｜一般行為

rect 直立

❶ rectangle ▸ rect + angle（角）

n. 長方形

例：The bag in the shape of a rectangle looks amazing.
那個長方形的包包看起來好美。

❷ rectify ▸ rect + ify（動詞字尾）

n. 改正，修改，矯正

例：I really hope this facility can rectify my brother's misconduct.
我真的希望這個場所可以矯正我弟弟的不當行為。

❸ correct ▸ cor（一起）+ rect

adj. 正確的，準確的 v. 改正，改錯

例：The answer is correct! Congratulation! You won the big prize!
答案是正確的！恭喜你！你贏得了大獎！

❹ direct ▸ di(away) + rect

v. 指向，指揮，命令，指導 adj. 率直的，直接的，直達的 adv. 直接地

例：The blockbuster was directed by Lily Lin.
這部賣座大片是由莉莉林拍攝的。

❺ erect ▸ e（向外的= out）+ rect

adj. 直立的，直立的 v. 使直立，建立

例：The government intended to erect a monument in front of the park.
政府打算在公園前建立一個紀念碑。

reg 治理

❶ region ▶ reg + ion （名詞字尾）

n. 地方，地域，地帶，區域，部位

例：The region was infested with mosquitoes. 這個地區飽受蚊子侵擾。

❷ regular ▶ reg + ular

adj. 規則的，井然有序的，定期的 n. 正規士兵，常客

例：I'd like to have regular working hours than being a freelancer.
我喜歡規律的上班時間，勝過自由接案。

❸ regulate ▶ reg + ul + ate

v. （通過規則）控制，調整，管理，調節

例：This machine can regulate the fluctuating heat and make it stable.
這台機器可以調節浮動的熱氣，使其保持穩定。

❹ regime ▶ reg + ime

n. 政體，政權

例：The glory of the regime remained for centuries.
此政體的榮耀維持了數百年。

❺ regal ▶ reg + al

adj. 帝王的，王室的，莊嚴堂皇的

例：In many countries, eagles represent regal power.
在許多國中，老鷹代表著王權。

Part 4｜一般行為

scribe 寫

❶ ascribe ▶ a(to) + scribe

v. 歸因於……，歸咎於

例：The outbreak of the disease can be ascribed to the untransparency of information. 疫情的爆發可以被歸因於資訊不透明。

❷ describe ▶ de(down) + scribe

v. 描述，描寫

例：Can you briefly described your idea before we proceed to the presentation? 在進行簡報之前，你可以先簡短描述一下你的想法嗎？

❸ inscribe ▶ in(into) + scribe

v. （在石碑、金屬板、紙等上）刻寫

例：My father inscribed my mother's name on the wood panel.
我爸爸將我媽媽的名字刻在木板上。

❹ prescribe ▶ pre（預先的= before）+ scribe

v. 開處方

例：The doctor prescribed three weeks' medicine for my father.
醫生幫我爸爸開了三週的藥。

❺ subscribe ▶ sub（之下= under）+ scribe

v. 訂閱

例：If you are interested in the videos to come, please subscribe to my channel! 如果你對之後的影片有興趣，請訂閱我的頻道！

rupt 打斷

❶ abrupt ▶ ab（偏離= away）+ rupt

adj. 突然的，意外的

例：The abrupt sound of lightening scared everyone in the room.
突如其來的雷響嚇到了房間裡所有人。

❷ bankrupt ▶ bank + rupt

adj. 破產的 v. 使破產 n. 破產的人

例：The company finally went bankrupt after years of deficit.
在連年虧損之後，這間公司最終宣告破產了。

❸ corrupt ▶ cor（一起的= together）+ rupt

adj. 墮落的，不道德的，收取賄賂的

例：The corrupt government was overthrown at the end.
腐敗的政府最終被推翻了。

❹ disrupt ▶ dis(away) + rupt

v. 使分裂，使瓦解，使中斷 adj. 中斷的，破裂的

例：The accident disrupted the already-busy traffic.
意外使本來就很繁忙的交通中斷了。

❺ interrupt ▶ inter（之間= between）+ rupt

v. 打斷，妨礙，打擾

例：It's rude to interrupt people when they're making a comment.
在他人發表評論的時候打斷他們是無禮的。

Part 4｜一般行為

sign 符號

❶ signify ▸ sign + ify（動詞字尾）

v.（用話、信號等）表示，意味

例：The white flag signified that the enemy had surrendered.
白旗表示敵方投降了。

❷ assign ▸ as(to) + sign

v. 分配，指定，委派

例：We were assigned different experiments in the class.
在這堂課中我們被分配做不同的實驗。

❸ consign ▸ con（一起= together）+ sign

v. 交付，委託，托運

例：The little baby was consigned and later adopted by the kind couple.
這個小孩被交付給那對善心夫婦，並於最後被領養。

❹ design ▸ de(down) + sign

v./n. 構想，計畫，設計

例：Our manager asked us to design a new layout for the building.
我們經理要我們重新設計大樓的格局。

❺ resign ▸ re(again) + sign

v. 辭職

例：I hated this job, so Idecided to resign at the end of the month.
我厭惡這份工作，所以我決定在月底離職。

Part 4 | 一般行為

spect 看

❶ spectacle ▸ spect + acle

n. 景象，奇觀，場面

例：The gathering was such an astounding spectacle.
這場集會真是令人瞠目結舌的景象。

❷ spectator ▸ spect + ator（表示人）

n. 觀眾，觀看的人

例：The spectators were all amazed by the brilliant Broadway show.
這場傑出的百老匯演出讓所有觀眾感到驚奇。

❸ spectacular ▸ spect + acular

adj. 壯觀的，奇景的

例：The mountain scenery is so spectacular that we all stop to appreciate the view. 山景是那麼壯觀，我們都停下腳步欣賞風景。

❹ aspect ▸ a(to) + spect

n. 見解，（事物的）外觀，情況，局面

例：We need to look into this matter from a new aspect to solve the problem. 我們必須用一個新的角度來看這個問題以解決它。

❺ inspect ▸ in(into) + spect

v. 調查，視察

例：The police patrolled and inspected the neighborhood with great caution. 警方謹慎地巡邏並視察社區。

❻ introspect ▶ intro（向內=inward）+ spect

v. 內省，內觀

例：From time to time, we need to introspect and reflect on our life.
有時候，我們需要內省並反思我們的人生。

❼ prospect ▶ pro（向前的 = forth）+ spect

n. 預想的事，期待，前景，可能性 v. 勘探

例：The prospect of graduation in just a month excited me.
一想到一個月內就要畢業了，我興奮不已。

❽ respect ▶ re(again) + spect

v. 尊敬，尊重 n. 尊敬

例：Show some respect to your parents and behave!
尊重你的父母，注意你的行為！

❾ suspect ▶ su(s)（之下= under）+ spect

v. 猜想，懷疑 n. 嫌疑犯 adj. 不可信的，可疑的

例：The authorities concerned suspected that the information was fake.
相關當局懷疑，此消息可能是假的。

❿ expect ▶ ex（向外= out）+ (s)pect

v. 期待，期望

例：I hope to meet him soon, but time is dragging.
我希望能盡快見到他，但時間過得好慢。

sist 站立

❶ assist ▸ as（朝向= to）+ sist

v./n. 幫助，協助

例：Can you assist us in coming up with ideas for this project?
你能幫助我們發想此專案的點子嗎？

❷ consist ▸ con（一起=together）+ sist

v. 組成，構成

例：This presentation consisted of three main parts: introduction, analysis, and summary.
此報告由三個部分組成：前言、分析，以及結論。

❸ insist ▸ in(into) + sist

v. 堅持（某些主張、想法）

例：My mother insisted that I stayed at home during the quarantine.
我媽媽堅持我在隔離期間待在家裡。

❹ persist ▸ per（完全地=completely）+ sist

v. 堅持，持續

例：The heavy rain persisted for more than a week and caused many casualties. 暴雨持續超過一個禮拜，造成許多傷亡。

❺ resist ▸ re(against) + sist

v. 抵抗，反抗，耐（熱、酸等）

例：If we continue to resist the dictatorship, our revolution will succeed one day. 若我們持續反抗獨裁政權，我們的革命某一天就會成功。

Part 4｜一般行為

ten、tin、tain 握持

❶ tenacious ▸ ten + ac(y) + ious（形容詞字尾）

adj. 固執的，堅韌的，頑強的

例：He grabbed my hand with a tenacious grip when I almost fell off the cliff.

在我快要掉下懸崖時，他緊緊地抓住了我的手。

❷ attain ▸ at（朝向= to）+ tain

v. 獲得，達成

例：Our goal is to attain this aim that everyone gets a mask to wear everyday.

我們的目標是達到每個人每天都有口罩可以帶。

❸ contain ▸ con（一起的= together）+ tain

v. 包含，抑制

例：All of our meals contain one appetizer, main dish, soup, and dessert.

我們所有的餐點都包含一份開胃菜、主餐、湯，以及點心。

❹ detain ▸ de(down) + tain

v. 扣留，留住

例：Those who broke the quarantine regulations will be detained by the police.

任何違反隔離規定的人都會被警方拘留。

❺ entertain ▶ enter（同 inter，之間=between）+ tain

V. 使愉快，款待，娛樂

例：I entertain myself by reading, writing, and listening to music.
我透過閱讀、寫作，以及聽音樂得到很大的享受。

❻ maintain ▶ main（同 man，手= hand）+ tain

V. 維持，保持，維持

例：Maintaining a healthy relationship requires great efforts and patience.
維持一段健康的感情需要大量的努力和耐心。

❼ obtain ▶ ob（表強調）+ tain

V. 獲取，得到

例：I obtain a great sense of satisfaction by helping others.
透過幫助別人，我得到很大的滿足感。

❽ sustain ▶ sus（之下=under）+ tain

V. 維持

例：We need water to sustain life; hence, any form of water pollution should be prohibited.
我們需要水來維持生命，所以任何形式的水污染都應該被禁止。

❾ continue ▶ con（一起的= together）+ tin + ue

V. 繼續，持續

例：Shall we continue the discussion?
我們繼續討論吧？

Part 4｜一般行為

tend 伸展

❶ tender ▶ tend + er（表人事物）

adj. 柔軟的，嫩的，溫柔的 v. 使變柔軟

例：Children's skins are usually very tender and got bruises easily.
小孩的肌膚通常都非常敏感，容易瘀青。

❷ attend ▶ at（朝向= to）+ tend

v. 參加，前往，照料（+ to）

例：It is mandatory to attend the annual meeting this Friday afternoon.
每個人都必須參加這星期五下午的年度會議。

❸ distend ▶ dis(away) + tend

v. 使膨脹，擴張

例：The distended veins we discovered during the autopsy indicated that the man took drugs.
在驗屍過程中發現的腫脹血管顯示該名男子吸毒。

❹ extend ▶ ex（向外= out）+ tend

v. 拉開，延長，伸展，伸出

例：We should extend the fences so that they enclose the whole farmland. 我們應該延展圍籬，使其能完整包圍農地。

❺ intend ▶ in(into) + tend

v. 打算，意圖，意味

例：I intended to go to Germany as an exchange student next semester. 我打算下學期去德國當交換學生。

Part 4｜一般行為

tract 拖拉

❶ tractable ▸ tract + able（可以的）

adj. 易處理的，易於管教的，易駕馭的

例：The docile and tractable horse is the mascot of the farm.
那匹溫馴的馬是這座農場的吉祥物。

❷ abstract ▸ abs（離開 = off）+ tract

adj. 抽象的，深奧的 n. 概要，抽象的概念

例：Please rewrite your abstract. It's hard to understand and that makes it useless.
請重寫你的摘要。太難理解了，等於沒用。

❸ attract ▸ at（朝向= to）+ tract

v. 吸引，引起注意

例：I was deeply attracted by the man who goes through all the pain but still chooses to be gentle and kind to others.
我被那名男子深深吸引，儘管經歷過所有通苦，他仍選擇以善意溫柔待人。

❹ contract ▸ con（一起的= together）+ tract

n. 合約，約定，得病 v. 簽約，約定，承辦

例：Let's sign the contract now, shall we?
我們現在就簽訂合約吧，如何？

⑤ distract ▶ dis（遠離= away）+ tract

v. 轉移，使分心

例：The film distracted me from preparing for the final exam.
電影使我無法專注準備期末考。

⑥ extract ▶ ex（向外的= out）+ tract

v. 取出，提取，提煉，榨取，摘錄 n. 提取物，摘錄

例：The facial cream is made from the extracts of roses.
這款臉霜是由玫瑰萃取物製作而成的。

⑦ protract ▶ pro（向前的 = forth）+ tract

v. 拖拉，延長

例：Is it possible that we protract the meeting since we haven't reached a conclusion?
因為還沒達成結論，有可能我們延長會議嗎？

⑧ retract ▶ re（往回= back）+ tract

v. 縮回，撤回

例：The wolf retraced his teeth and dropped the body of the deer.
狼縮回牙齒，丟下鹿的屍體。

⑨ subtract ▶ sub（之下= under）+ tract

v. 減去，減掉

例：Subtract 5 from 5 and the sum is 0. 五減五總結是零。

ven、vent 來

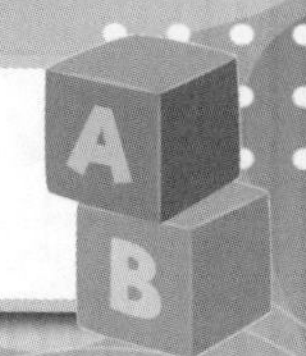

❶ advent ▶ ad（向）+ vent

n. 到來，出現

例：Since the advent of Industrial Revolution, the society has been changing in a fast pace. 從工業革命開始，社會快速變遷。

❷ adventure ▶ ad（向）+ vent + ure

v./n. 冒險

例：Let's take an adventure and go on a road trip!
我們來場冒險，去公路旅行吧！

❸ event ▶ e（向外 = out）+ vent

n. 事件

例：The terrible event occurred because all of us weren't careful enough. 這起可怕的事件會發生都是因為我們不夠謹慎。

❹ invent ▶ in + vent

v. 發明，創造

例：The scientist invented a clock that was said to have to power to turn back time. 這名科學家發明了一個時鐘，據說它能讓時間倒流。

❺ prevent ▶ pre（之前 = before）+ vent

v. 防止，阻止，預防

例：To prevent further infection, all indoor gatherings exceeding 100 people are banned.
為了防止進一步感染，所有室內超過一百人的集會都會被禁止。

❻ venue ▸ ven + ue

n. 地點，會場

例：Please arrive at the venue of the convention on time.
請準時到達研討會的會場。

❼ convene ▸ con（一起 = together）+ vene

v. 召集，聚集

例：The president convened major business tycoons to make a nationwide rescue plan.
總統召集重量級商業巨頭，商討全國性的紓困計畫。

❽ revenue ▸ re(back) + ven + ue

n. 收益，收入

例：The revenue is decreasing, and we may go bankrupt soon.
收入持續減少，我們可能很快就會破產了。

❾ intervene ▸ inter（之間 = between）+ vene

v. 介入，干涉

例：He kept intervening in our argument, and most importantly, he wasn't helping.
他一直介入我們之間的爭論，而最重要的是，他一點忙也沒幫到。

tort 扭曲

❶ torture ▶ tort + ure

n./v. 拷問，折磨，痛苦

例：Waiting for the result of the exam to come out is such a torture.
等待考試結果出爐真是個折磨。

❷ contort ▶ con（一起 = together）+ tort

v. 曲解，扭曲，使變形

例：The metal contorted under high temperature.
金屬在高溫之中扭曲變形。

❸ distort ▶ dis（偏離 = away）+ tort

v. 曲解，扭曲

例：Don't distort my words. I didn't mean it that way.
別曲解我的話。我沒有那個意思。

❹ extort ▶ ex（向外 = out）+ tort

v. 勒索，敲詐，侵佔

例：How dare you to try to extort the president? 你怎麼敢勒索總統？

❺ retort ▶ re(again) + tort

v. 反駁，回嘴

例：My parents grew angrier and angrier when my brother kept retorting. 我弟弟一直回嘴，我爸媽越來越生氣。

Part 4｜一般行為

test 測試

❶ testify ▸ test + ify（動詞字尾）

v. 指證，作證

例：Are you willing to testify for Andy Dufresne?
你願意為安迪杜佛蘭作證嗎？

❷ testament ▸ test + a + ment

n. 遺囑，證明，舊約聖經

例：According to the testament, you are the only heiress to the property.
根據遺囑，你是此財產的唯一繼承人。

❸ contest ▸ con（一起= together）+ test

v. 爭奪，競爭，角逐 n. 比賽，競爭

例：If we don't become friends, we'll be contesting against each other.
我們如果做不成朋友，就是競爭對手了。

❹ detest ▸ de(not) + test

v. 厭惡，嫌惡

例：I detest the smell of mushrooms, carrots, and raw fish.
我厭惡蘑菇、紅蘿蔔，以及生魚的味道。

❺ protest ▸ pro（向前的= forth）+ test

v./n. 抗議，反對，聲明

例：The demonstrators continued to protest against the new labor law.
遊行人士持續針對新勞基法進行抗議。

Part 4｜一般行為

turb 擾亂

❶ turbine ▸ turb + ine

n. 渦輪機

例：The turbine stopped working. Can you get mom to fix it?
渦輪機停止運作了，你可以叫媽媽來修理嗎？

❷ turbid ▸ turb + id（表狀態）

adj. 渾濁的，混亂的

例：The turbid river was the result of mismanagement from the authorities concerned.
這條河流之所以會那麼渾濁，是因為有關當局並未妥善管理。

❸ turbulent ▸ turb + ul + ent

adj. 騷亂的，狂暴的，混亂的

例：This era was particularly turbulent due to corruptions, diseases, and low level of hygiene.
因為腐敗、疾病，和低衛生程度，這個時代特別動盪混亂。

❹ disturb ▸ dis（反向= away）+ turb

v. 妨礙，打擾，弄亂

例：Mom is working. Don't disturb her. 媽媽在工作，不要打擾她。

❺ perturb ▸ per（徹底的= completely）+ turb

v. 使不安，使慌張，煩擾

例：The scandal perturbed the whole organizational operation for quite a while. 此弊案擾亂組織運作好一陣子。

vert、vers 轉向

❶ avert ▸ a（朝向= toward）+ vert

v. 避開，防止

例：We can avert our eyes from a scene, but we can't avoid the spontaneous feelings.
我們可以避開視線，卻無法不面對油然而生的感受。

❷ convert ▸ con（一起 = together）+ vert

v. 改變，變換，改變宗教信仰

例：My mom converted to Christianity for my father.
我媽媽為了我爸爸改信基督教。

❸ divert ▸ di（偏離 =away）+ vert

v. 轉移，改道

例：The government diverted the main road to ease the heavy traffic flow. 政府將主要道路改線，舒緩大車流量。

❹ invert ▸ in(into) + vert

v. 使顛倒，使轉換 adj. 顛倒的

例：Invert the words backward, and you'll see that it's actually a Chinese character.
將字母顛倒過來，你會發現它其實是中文字母。

❺ revert ▸ re(back) + vert

v. 返回，復原

例：The speaker reverted to the issue of sustainable energy and added more explanations.
講者又回到永續能源的問題，並多做了解釋。

❻ subvert ▸ sub(under) + vert

v. 顛覆，推翻

例：The armed force subverted the government instead, and established a warlord regime. 軍隊反而顛覆政府，建立了軍閥政權。

❼ adverse ▸ ad(to) + verse(turn)

adj. 不利的，敵對的，反面的

例：The adverse weather escalated the level of difficulty during the shipment. 險惡的天氣加深了運輸的難度。

❽ diverse ▸ di（偏離= away）+ verse

adj. 多種多樣的，多元的

例：A diverse curriculum is beneficial to the overall education of children. 多元化的課綱對小孩的整體教育來説是有益的。

❾ universe ▸ uni（一 = one）+ verse

n. 宇宙

例：The universe is still expanding, and I firmly believe there are aliens out there. 宇宙仍在擴張，我深信有外星人在那。

vict、vinc 征服

❶ victory ▶ vict + ory

n. 勝利，克服，征服

例：The team won consecutive victories in the championship!
該隊在錦標賽中獲得連勝！

❷ convince ▶ con（連同 = with）+ vince

v. 說服，使明白

例：You have to convince me first before you proceed to the CEO.
在去找總裁之前，你得先說服我。

❸ convict ▶ con（一起 =together）+ vict

v. 證明……有罪，判決 n. 罪犯

例：He was convicted of murder and jailed for life.
她因謀殺被判有罪，服終生刑期。

❹ evince ▶ e（向外 = out）+ vince

v. 表明（感情），顯示

例：We can tell that Red evinced great regrets when he filed for parole.
瑞德在申請假釋時，我們可以看到他展現極大的懊悔。

❺ evict ▶ e（往外 = out）+ vict

v. 驅逐，逐出，趕出

例：They are evicted out of the hotel for making loud noises.
他們因為製造噪音被趕出旅館。

Part 5 | 性質特色

acro 高

❶ acrobatics ▸ acro + bat + ics（學說）

n. 雜技（表演），技巧

例：Acrobatics takes decades to practice.
雜技演出需要好幾十年的練習。

❷ acrophobia ▸ acro + phob（恐懼 = fear）+ ia（病態）

n. 恐高症

例：I have acrophobia. That's why I hate suspensions.
我有懼高症，這就是為什麼我討厭吊橋。

❸ acropolis ▸ acro + polis（城市 = city）

n. 衛城

例：Roaming on the top of the acropolis made all of us nostalgic.
在衛城上漫步讓我們所有人感到一股鄉愁。

❹ acronym ▸ acro + (o)nym（名字 = name）

n. 首字母縮略詞

例：WHO is the acronym of World Health Organization.
WHO 是世界衛生組織的縮寫。

❺ acrogen ▸ acro + gen（產生 = birth）

n. 頂生植物

例：A fern or moss is the most common known acrogen.
蕨類或是苔蘚是最為人熟知的頂生植物。

bell 好戰的，戰爭

❶ rebellious ▶ re(back) + bell + ious（形容詞字尾）

adj. 造反的，反叛的

例：The rebellious troop gathered in front of the hall to declare war.
反叛軍集結在會堂前宣戰。

❷ belligerent ▶ belli + ger（從事 = wage）+ ent

adj. 交戰中的，好戰的 n. 交戰國

例：The belligerent nations hold a secret meeting and agreed to call a truce. 交戰國舉行了秘密會議，宣布休戰。

❸ antebellum ▶ ante（之前的 = before）+ bell + um

adj.（美國南北戰爭）戰爭前的

例：The antebellum era was said to be filled with hunger, chaos, and corruption. 戰前時代據說無處不是飢荒、混亂，以及腐敗。

❹ rebellion ▶ re(back) + bell + ion（名詞字尾）

n. 反抗，反叛，叛亂

例：The protagonist's rebellion against fate in the movie was a real tear-jerker. 這部電影中主角對命運的反抗真是賺人熱淚。

❺ rebel ▶ re(back) + bel

n. 反叛者，造反者 v. 造反，反叛

例：Finally, the people rebelled against the dictator and overthrew the government. 最終，人民起身反抗獨裁者，推翻了政府。

carn 肉

❶ carnal ▸ carn + al

adj. 肉體的，世俗的，肉欲的，淫蕩的

例：Carnal desires are hard to resist for most of people.
身體慾望對大多數人來說都是很難抗拒的。

❷ carnivorous ▸ carn(i) + vor（吃 = eat）+ ous

adj. 肉食性的

例：Human beings, like most of other animals, are carnivorous.
人類就像大多數其他動物一樣，都是肉食性的。

❸ incarnation ▸ in(into) + carn + ation（名詞字尾）

n. 體現，化身

例：I seriously think that the baby is the incarnation of my dog.
我認真覺得這嬰兒是我狗狗的化身。

❹ carnage ▸ carn + age（集合名詞字尾）

n. 殺戮，大屠殺

例：We can only hope that if the third world war were to happen, there wouldn't be any carnage.
我們只能祈禱，若第三次世界大戰真的來臨，不會有大屠殺發生。

❺ carnation ▸ carn + ation

n. 肉色，粉紅色，康乃馨 adj. 肉色的

例：I brought my mother a bouquet of carnation on Mother's Day.
我在母親節那天買了康乃馨給我媽媽。

Part 5｜性質特色

crypt、cond 隱密的、藏的

❶ cryptic ▸ crypt + ic（形容詞字尾）

adj. 隱密的，秘密的，神秘的

例：The cryptic notes kept by the priest were believed to be the truth of the scandal. 神父所持有的秘密手記被認為藏有醜聞的真相。

❷ cryptogram ▸ crypto + gram（書寫）

n. 密文，密碼

例：The government hired a professional to decode the cryptogram.
政府雇用一名專家解密此密文。

❸ cryptography ▸ crypto + graphy（紀錄）

n. 密碼學，使用密碼的方式

例：Fascinated by The Da Vinci Code, Dan decided to choose cryptography as his major.
丹深受《達文西密碼》吸引，因此選了密碼學當作主修。

❹ abscond ▸ abs（遠離 = away） + cond

v. 潛逃，逃亡

例：The prisoners absconded to Mexico when the government was busy dealing with the disease control.
在政府忙於控制疫情時，囚犯潛逃至墨西哥。

❺ recondite ▸ re(back) + cond + ite（表性質）

adj. 深奧的，難理解的，隱秘的

例：*The Theory of Time* was his more recondite work, compared to his previous ones.
相較於先前的作品，《時間理論》是他更為深奧難懂的著作。

Part 5｜性質特色

dur 持續

❶ during ▶ dur + ing

prep. 在……期間，在……的時候

例：During the quarantine, you are not allowed to leave home.
在隔離期間，你不允許外出。

❷ durable ▶ dur + able（可以的）

adj. 耐用的，耐久的 n. 耐用品

例：The desk is rather durable; we've been using it for decades.
這個桌子相當耐用，我們已經用了好幾十年了。

❸ endure ▶ en（使）+ dure

v. 堅持，忍耐，持久

例：I can't endure to see the old man suffering this much pain.
我不忍看到這個老人承受這般痛苦。

❹ obdurate ▶ ob（對抗 = against）+ dur + ate

adj. 頑固的，固執的

例：Obdurate and opinionated, the man was finally laid off.
又頑固又專制，男子終於被開除了。

❺ duration ▶ dur + ation（名詞字尾）

n. 持續，持續時間

例：The duration of the session lasts for 4 hours.
這場會議將持續四個小時。

Part 5｜性質特色

equa、equi 相同的

❶ equal ▶ equ + al

adj. 相同的，能勝任的，同等的 v. 相等，比得上 n. 相同的人事物

例：All men are equal, and no one deserves to be treated less.
所有人都是平等的，沒有人值得被惡劣對待。

❷ equator ▶ equ + at(e) + or（表人事物）

n. 赤道

例：The village near the Equator is abundant in wild sunflowers.
那座在赤道邊的村莊擁有許多向日葵。

❸ equilibrium ▶ equi + libr（平橫 = balance） + ium（狀態）

n. 平衡，均衡，均勢

例：Your major task is to maintain the supply-demand equilibrium.
你的主要任務就是維持供需平衡。

❹ equinox ▶ equi + nox（夜晚= night）

n. 晝夜平分之時

例：The autumn equinox of 2020 falls on September 22.
2020 年的秋分是在9 月22 號。

❺ equivalent ▶ equi + val（價值= worth）+ ent

adj. 相等的，等值的 n. 對等物，等量，對應詞

例：His response is equivalent to a silent approval, so go head and finish the task. 他的回應等同於默許，所以去做吧，完成任務。

fid 相信

❶ fidelity ▸ fidel + ity（名詞字尾）

n. 忠實，忠誠

例：When you questioned my fidelity, the trust between us was broken.
當你質疑我的忠誠時，我們之間的信任就破裂了。

❷ confide ▸ con（一起 = together）+ fide

v. 吐露，委託，信賴

例：My parents confided in me and I never disappointed them.
我們父母信任我，而我也從未讓他們失望。

❸ diffident ▸ dif（遠離 = away）+ fid + ent

adj. 缺乏自信的，羞怯的

例：Far from being pretentious, she's rather diffident about giving comments. 她一點都不自視甚高，反而在發表意見時相當沒有自信。

❹ perfidy ▸ per（徹底地 = completely）+ fidy

n. 背信，不忠

例：The perfidy of his wife utterly wracked him.
她妻子的不忠讓他一蹶不振。

❺ infidelity ▸ in（表否定）+ fidel + ity

n. 不忠誠，背叛

例：Infidelity and dishonesty are not allowed in our marriage.
背叛和不誠實在我們的婚姻之中是不被允許的。

Part 5｜性質特色

firm 堅定的

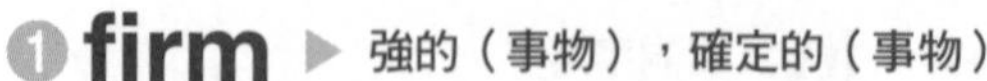

❶ firm ▶ 強的（事物），確定的（事物）

adj. 堅固的，牢固的，堅決的 adv. 穩固地 v. 使穩固，使確定
n. 公司，商號

例：The foundation is not firm enough to withstand a building of this weight. 地基不夠穩固，無法承受這般重量的建物。

❷ affirm ▶ af(to) + firm

v. 斷言，肯定，證實

例：Tommy can affirm that Andy wasn't the murderer of his wife.
湯米可以證實安迪並沒有謀殺他的妻子。

❸ confirm ▶ con（一起 = with） + firm

v. 確認，批准

例：I need you to confirm the budget before we execute the plan.
我需要你批准預算，我們才能執行計畫。

❹ infirm ▶ in（表否定） + firm

adj. 虛弱的，意志薄弱的

例：An infirm mind is what leads him to this situation now.
意志薄弱是它落到此地步的原因。

❺ reaffirm ▶ re(again) + af(to) + firm

v. 重申

例：I reaffirm: no one is permitted to leave home during the quarantine.
我重申一次：在隔離期間，沒有人可以外出。

neg 否定

❶ negate ▶ neg + ate（動詞字尾）

v. 否定，否認，取消，使無效

例：Why do you have to negate all my efforts just because I made one single mistake?
為什麼只因為我犯了一個錯誤，你就要否定我所有的努力？

❷ neglect ▶ neg + lect（選擇 = choose）

v./n. 忽視，忽略

例：Mandy was neglecting me because I told the professor that she cheated on the exam.
曼蒂正在無視我，因為我告訴教授她在考試中作弊。

❸ negotiate ▶ neg + oti（閒散的）+ ate

v. 協商，交涉，談判

例：I'm here representing my company to negotiate the deal.
我在此代表我們公司協商交易。

❹ abnegate ▶ ab（遠離= away）+ neg + ate

n. 棄權，否認

例：The Queen abnegated her loyal powers to her only child.
皇后將王全交給她唯一的孩子。

❺ negative ▶ neg + ative

adj. 負面的，消極的 n. 否定，拒絕，底片

例：The tests for coronavirus were negative. What a great relief.
新型肺炎檢測為陰性，真是鬆了一口氣。

part 部分

❶ partial ▸ part + ial

adj. 部分的，局部的，不公平的，偏袒的

例：The professor is clearly partial to students with high academic performance.
教授很顯然比較偏袒成績好的學生。

❷ partake ▸ part + (t)ake

v. 參與，參加，分擔

例：All students and teachers are required to partake in the disease control speech.
所有學生和老師都必須參加防疫演講。

❸ participate ▸ part + i + cip（拿取 = take）+ ate

v. 參加，參與，分享

例：I don't feel like participating in the competition due to my illness.
因為生病，我不想參加這個比賽。

❹ particle ▸ part+i + cle（小的事物）

n. 極小量，顆粒，粒子

例：We can see particles of sand scattered on the floor here and there.
我們可以觀察到沙粒散亂在房間裡。

❺ participle ▶ part + i + cip（拿取 = take）+ le

n. 分詞

例：Use participles when you want to separate two sentences.
想要將兩個句子分開時，使用分詞。

❻ apart ▶ a（遠離 = away）+ part

adv. 分開地，遠離的，單獨地

例：The memorial park and the bar are only two miles apart.
紀念公園和酒吧只隔了兩英里。

❼ compartment ▶ com（共同）+ part + ment

n. 隔間，劃分 v. 分隔

例：The new high-speed train has more than 20 compartments for VIPs.
新的高速火車提供了超過二十個隔間給貴賓使用。

❽ depart ▶ de(down) + part

v. 出發，離開，啟程

例：We'll depart at 10 a.m. sharp, for we don't want to get stuck in the traffic.
我們會準時十點離開，因為我們不想遇到塞車。

❾ impartial ▶ im（表否定）+ partial

adj. 公正的，不偏不倚的

例：The judges vowed to be impartial during the contest.
評審鄭重宣告在比賽中保持中立。

Part 5｜性質特色

nov、neo 新的

❶ novel ▸ nov + el

adj. 新穎的，稀奇的 n. （長篇）小說

例：The novel ideas in this proposal won the board's approval.
提案中的新穎想法獲得了董事會的批准。

❷ novice ▸ nov + ice（動作之人）

n. 初學者，新手

例：I'm a novice here, working for only a few months.
我是個新手，在這裡只工作了幾個月。

❸ innovate ▸ in(into) + nov + ate（使）

v. 革新，改革，創新

例：The RD department was trying to innovate a new system that improves efficiency. 研發部門正試著做出創新系統，提升效能。

❹ renovate ▸ re(again) + nov + ate（使）

v. 更新，修復，革新

例：I think our living room need some renovating. What do you think?
我覺得我們的客廳可以重新修繕一下，你覺得如何？

❺ neolithic ▸ neo + lith（石頭）+ ic

adj. 新石器時代的

例：Those Neolithic relics exhibited the living traces of our ancestors.
這些新石器時代的遺跡展示出我們祖先的生活足跡。

para 旁邊

❶ parenthesis ▶ par + en(into) + thesis（放置）

n. 插入語

例：Make sure you use the parenthesis in pairs.
使用插入語時，記得前後都要有。

❷ paragraph ▶ para + graph（書寫）

n. 段落 v. 分段

例：We were asked to translated respective paragraphs into English.
我們被要求將個別段落翻譯成英文。

❸ paraphrase ▶ para + phrase（語句）

v. 釋義，用不同的方式重新說一次 n. 釋義，意譯，解釋

例：Can you paraphrase your statement? It's a little confusing for all of us. 你可以重述你的發言嗎？我們覺得有點困惑。

❹ parasite ▶ para + site（地方）

n. 寄生蟲，寄生生物

例：In Africa, most of the diseases were caused by parasites in polluted water. 在非洲，許多疾病是由污水中的寄生蟲所造成的。

❺ paradigm ▶ para + digm（範例：= example）

n. 典範，範例

例：I'm proud to say that my father set a paradigm of dignity, maturity, and independence. 我很自豪地說，我爸爸是尊嚴、成熟，以及獨立的典範。

Part 5｜性質特色

simul、simil 相似

❶ similar ▸ simil + ar

adj. 像……的，類似的

例：This product is quite similar to your previous one. Why should I buy it? 這個產品和你們之前的很像。為什麼我要買它？

❷ simile ▸ simil + e

n. （修辭）明喻

例：To directly describe one's blushing cheeks as roses is to employ simile. 直接將一個人害羞的臉頰比喻成玫瑰即是使用明喻。

❸ simulate ▸ simul + ate（使）

v. 模擬，模仿 adj. 假裝的，模擬的

例：This laboratory tests new AI products in simulated situations.
此實驗室在模擬情境中測試人工智慧產品。

❹ assimilate ▸ as(to) + simil + ate（使）

v. 同化，使相同，吸收

例：Mathematics contains too many formulas that are hard for me to assimilate. 數學有太多公式是我很難吸收的。

❺ simultaneous ▸ simul + tane（時間 = time）+ ous

adj. 同時發生的，同步的

例：Simultaneous translation requires years of training and practical experiences. 同步翻譯需要好幾年的訓練和實戰經驗。

Part 5｜性質特色

term、termin 結束、界線

❶ terminal ▶ termin + al

adj. 最末的，終點的，最終的 n. 結尾，終點，末端，終站

例：The remaining passengers all got off at the terminal station.
剩餘的乘客都在終點站下車了。

❷ terminate ▶ termin + ate（使）

v. 使結束，使終止

例：Our contract will terminate at the end of March.
我們的合約會在三月底到期。

❸ determine ▶ de(down) + termin + e

v. 下決心，做出決定

例：I'm determined to obtain my master's degree in two years.
我下定決心要在兩年內拿到碩士學位。

❹ exterminate ▶ ex（往外= out）+ termin + ate

v. 根除，消滅

例：We all hope that the pills can exterminate the rats in this building for good. 我們都希望這款藥可以永久讓老師在大樓中絕跡。

❺ conterminous ▶ con（一起的 = with）+ termin + ous

adj. 連接的，相連的

例：The 3 conterminous neighborhoods form a circle, and the city hall is located at the middle.
這三個相連的社區形成一個圓環，市中心就坐落在中間。

Part 6｜自然元素

aero 空氣

❶ aerobatics ▸ aero + bat + ics（技術）

n. 特技飛行，特技飛行術

例：The amazing performance of the aerobatics entertained all the foreign guests. 特技飛行的精彩演出讓外賓感到滿足。

❷ aerial ▸ aer(o) + ial

adj. 空氣的，大氣的，飄渺的，高聳的

例：Aerial yoga involves high-intensity muscle workout and antigravity training. 空中瑜伽需要高強度肌肉運動和反重力訓練。

❸ aerate ▸ aer(o) + ate（使）

v. 使充滿空氣，暴露於空氣中

例：Aerating the lawn before you plant the seeds is crucial.
在播種之前鬆土是很重要的。

❹ aeroplane ▸ aero + plane（飛機）

n. 飛機

例：The government invested billions of US dollars to build this giant aeroplane. 政府投資百億美金建造大型飛機。

❺ aeronautics ▸ aero + naut（航行 = sail）+ ics（知識）

adj. 航空學，飛行術

例：He studied hard and trained himself as an expert in the field of aeronautics. 他努力讀書，並訓練自己成為航空學領域的專家。

Part 6 | 自然元素

agro、agri、agra 土地

❶ agrarian ▶ agra + rian（相關的）

adj. 土地的，農田的，農業的 n. 平均地權論者

例：According to the historical record, the agrarian society flourished for centuries. 根據歷史記載，這個農業社會繁華了數百年。

❷ agriculture ▶ agri + cult（耕種）+ ure

n. 農業，農耕

例：The country relies heavily on agriculture, accounting for nearly half of its GDP. 這個國家相當倚重農業，其占了GDP將近一半。

❸ agronomy ▶ agro + nomy（學科）

n. 農學，農藝學

例：Knowing only how to grow rice doesn't mean you're skilled in agronomy. 只懂得種米不代表你熟稔農藝學。

❹ agribusiness ▶ agri + business（產業）

n. 農業相關產業

例：Agribusiness management is a rather popular major these days. 農企業管理近年來是相當熱門的主修科系。

❺ agrochemical ▶ agro + chemical（化學的）

n. 農用化學品

例：The agrochemical company sold pesticides that do not match the standard to farmers, and was fined for 1 million dollars. 這個農用化學品公司販售不合規定的除蟲劑給農夫，最後被罰了一百萬元。

Part 6 | 自然元素

aqua 水

❶ aquarium ▶ aqua + rium（表地方）

n. 水族館

例：We went to the aquarium and listend to the tour guide.
我們去水族館聽導覽。

❷ aquatic ▶ aqu(a) + atic（有某性質的）

adj. 水的，水中的，水生的 n. 水生植物，水生動物

例：Some aquatic plants are not easy-to-grow and survive only in the ocean. 有些水生植物並不好種植，只能在海洋裡生存。

❸ aqueduct ▶ aque + duct（引導 = lead）

n. 導水管，管道

例：The ancient aqueduct was secretly demolished by the government at night. 這個古蹟渠道在晚上被政府秘密拆除了。

❹ aqualung ▶ aqua + lung（肺）

n. （潛水用）水中呼吸器，水肺

例：Aqualung is an underwater breathing gear that introduces scuba diving to the world. 水肺是將水肺潛水帶向世界的水下呼吸設備。

❺ aquaculture ▶ aqua + cult（耕種）+ ure

n. 水產養殖

例：This scientific research certainly made contributions to the development of aquaculture.
此科學研究確實替水產養殖的發展做出了貢獻。

astro、aster 星

❶ asterisk ▸ aster + isk（小的 = small）

n. 星號 v. 加星號於

例：The main statement was marked with an asterisk; it's easy to spot.
重點論述已經用星號標記起來了；很容易就能找到。

❷ astronomy ▸ astro + nomy（治理）

n. 天文學

例：Before you become an astronaut, you need to master astronomy first. 在成為一名太空人之前，你必須先精通天文學。

❸ astronaut ▸ astro + naut（航行之人 = sailor）

n. 太空人

例：The astronaut made a remarkable discovery and solved the mystery of the universe. 該名太空人做出驚人發現，解開了宇宙之秘。

❹ asteroid ▸ aster + oid（像某物的）

n. 小行星 adj. 星狀的

例：The asteroid eventually fell on the plain and made a blast.
小行星最後轟然一響，掉到大平原上。

❺ disaster ▸ dis(away) + aster

n. 災難，不幸

例：The missile launch ended in disaster, meaning a waste of 1 billion dollars. 飛彈發射失敗，代表浪費了一百億元。

Part 6 | 自然元素

geo 地球、地理

❶ geography ▸ geo + graphy（紀錄）

n. 地理（學），（某個地方的）地理

例：The geography of the village made it a perfect fit for field research.
此村莊的地理位置使其成為田野調查的絕佳對象。

❷ geology ▸ geo + (o)logy（研究）

n. 地質學，地質

例：He also enrolled in a geology course to enhance his knowledge on geography. 為了加強對地理學的知識，他還修了地質學。

❸ geometry ▸ geo + metry（測量 = measure）

n. 幾何學

例：Analytic geometry is a required course in the Deparment of Mathemetics. 分析幾何學在數學系中是必修課。

❹ geographer ▸ geo + grap（書寫）+ er（表示人的字尾）

n. 地理學家

例：The geographer finally realized that the ancient city vanished because of the volcanic eruption.
此地理學家終於發現這座古老的城市是因為火山爆發而消失的。

❺ geographic ▸ geo + graph（書寫）+ ic（形容詞字尾）

adj. 地理學的；地理的

例：Geographic locations are defined by longitude and latitude.
地理位置是由經度和緯度決定的。

herb 草

❶ herb ▶ 表示草，主要指有益的草

n. 草，藥草

例：These herbs are proved to be clinically beneficial to bone strengthening. 這些藥草經臨床證實對骨骼強化有幫助。

❷ herbicide ▶ herbi + cide（殺 = kill）

n. 除草劑

例：Herbicide is now greatly discouraged to use by the public and the government. 社會和政府現今皆不鼓勵使用除草劑。

❸ herbivorous ▶ herbi + vor（吃 = eat）+ ous（形容詞字尾）

adj. 草食的，吃草的

例：Herbivorous animals feed on grass, plants, or algae.
草食性動物以草、植物，或是藻類為生。

❹ herbal ▶ herb + al（有某性質的）

adj. 草本的；藥草的

例：Herbal medicine requires both textbook knowledge and clinical experience. 草藥學不僅需要書本知識，也需要臨床經驗。

❺ herbarium ▶ herb + arium（表場所）

n. 植物標本集（室）

例：It's time that we make a new herbarium for this year's studies.
我們該替今年的研究做新的植物標本了。

Part 6｜自然元素

flor、flour 花

❶ floral ▶ flor + al（有關的）

adj. 花的，用花裝飾的

例：The floral patterns on the wedding dress is gorgeous.
婚紗上的花紋圖騰真美。

❷ floriculture ▶ flor + i + cult（耕種）+ ure

n. 花卉栽培

例：After retirement, my mother dedicated to floriculture and horticulture.
在退休之後，我媽媽將時間奉獻於花卉栽培和園藝。

❸ florid ▶ flor + id（有某性質的）

adj.（面容）紅潤的，玫瑰色的，（文體）華麗的

例：The florid complexion on the little girl's face reminded me of my childhood.
小女孩臉上紅潤的色澤讓我想起了我的童年。

❹ flourish ▶ flour + ish（動詞字尾）

v. 繁榮，興旺，蓬勃，茂盛 n. 興旺，揮動

例：Romanticism flourshed in the late 18th century.
浪漫主義興盛於十八世紀。

⑤ multiflorous ▸ multi（多的= many）+ flor + ous

adj. 多花的

例：Multiflorous plants, by definition, bear more than one flower during growth.
就定義來說，多花植物就是在生長期間盛開不只一朵花。

⑥ florescent ▸ flor + escent（形容詞字尾）

adj. 開花的，全盛的

例：The florescent period of plum blossoms usually start in winter.
梅花的全盛時間通常始於冬季。

Part 6｜自然元素

hydro、hydr 水

❶ hydrogen ▶ hydro + gen（產生= birth）

n. 氫

例：Hydrogen is one of the element to produce water.
氫是產出水的其中一個元素。

❷ hydrophobia ▶ hyrdo + phobia（恐懼）

n. 懼水症

例：Anyone having hydrophobia can choose other activities during the PE class. 任何有懼水症的人都可以在體育課中選擇其他活動。

❸ dehydrate ▶ de(down) + hydr + ate（使）

v. 使乾燥，脫水

例：I think I'm dehydrating. Can you give me a bottle of water?
我覺得我正在脫水。可以給我一瓶水嗎？

❹ hydrate ▶ hydr + ate（使）

n. 水合物 v. 使與水化合

例：The facial hydrating cream can moisturize your skin in a short time.
這個臉部飽水霜可以在短時間內滋潤你的肌膚。

❺ hydrant ▶ hydr + ant（表人事物）

n. 消火栓

例：The colors of hydrants actually indicate the amount of water the firefighters can use.
消防栓上的顏色事實上代表了消防員可以使用的水量。

mar 海洋

❶ marine ▸ mar + ine（有某性質的）

adj. 海的，海洋的 n. 海運，海軍陸戰隊

例：I am deeply attracted by the elegant moving style of marine animals. 我被海洋動物優美的移動姿態深深吸引。

❷ submarine ▸ sub（之下 = under）+ marine

n. 潛水艇 adj. 海底的，水下的

例：Living and working in a submarine requires extra practical training. 在潛水艇裡生活和工作需要額外的實地訓練。

❸ mariculture ▸ mari + cult（耕種）+ ure

n. 海洋生物養殖

例：Open sea mariculture is common in the Southern part of Taiwan. 外海水產養殖在台灣南部很常見。

❹ maritime ▸ mari + time

adj. 海的，海事的，沿海的

例：The two belligerent maritime powers agreed to cease the war. 這兩個交戰中的海上霸權同意停戰。

❺ aquamarine ▸ aqua + marine

n. 海藍寶石，淺綠色，海藍色

例：The aquamarine scene along Taitung's coastal line is simply breathtaking. 台東沿海岸湛藍的景象簡直讓人屏息。

Part 6 | 自然元素

luc、lumin、lustr 光

❶ lucid ▸ luc + id（表性質）

adj. 明晰的，易懂的，頭腦清醒的

例：Her lucid explanations enlightened the audience.
她清楚易懂的解釋讓觀眾豁然開朗。

❷ elucidate ▸ e(out) + lucid + ate（使）

v. 說明，闡明

例：You need to elucidate on your point of view since this is a brand-new project. 因為這是全新的專案，你需要多加闡述你的論點。

❸ luminous ▸ lumin + ous（形容詞字尾）

adj. 發光的，明亮的，清楚的

例：The organism turned out to be luminous in darkness.
此有機生物最後被發現可以在黑暗中發光。

❹ illuminate ▸ il(into) + lumin + ate（使）

v. （光）照亮，啟蒙，闡明

例：The pendulum illuminated the whole room with its warm light.
吊燈以其暖光照亮了整個房間。

❺ illustrate ▸ il(into) + lustr + ate（使）

v. （用實例、比較等）進行例證、插圖於（書籍等）

例：Do you mind illustrating more on the new theory of modern social structure? 你介意舉例說明此當代社會架構的新理論嗎？

phon、son 聲音

❶ phonetics ▶ phon + et（小的）+ ics（學問）

n. 語音學

例：Our professor said that studying phonetics can actually elevate one's English proficiency.
我們教授說，修習語音學事實上可以提升一個人的英語能力。

❷ euphony ▶ eu（好的 = good）+ phone + y

n. 悅耳之音，和諧的聲音

例：The woman's soothing tone made for an euphony when she read the poem. 女人柔和的聲調讓詩的朗誦非常悅耳。

❸ symphony ▶ sym（一起的 = same）+ phon + y

n. 交響樂，和諧

例：Stravinsky was not only a composer of symphonies but also a conductor. 史特拉文斯基不只是交響樂作曲家，也是指揮家。

❹ supersonic ▶ son + ic（表性質）

adj. 超音波的，超音速的 n. 超音波，超音速

例：The supersonic aircrafts were developed mainly for military use.
超音速飛機大多被研發作軍事用途。

❺ unison ▶ uni（一 = one）+ son

n. 和聲，協調

例：The choir sang in unison and created a peaceful atmosphere in the church. 合唱團齊合聲，在教堂內創造了平靜的氛圍。

Chapter 3
字尾 Suffix

ia、sis 疾病、病痛、症狀

❶ euthanasia ▸ eu（好的）+ thanas（死亡）+ ia

n. 安樂死

例：Euthanasia is still illegal in most Asian countries.
在大多數的亞洲國家中，安樂死仍屬非法。

❷ metastasis ▸ meta（改變）+ stasis

n. 轉移，新陳代謝

例：Cancer cell metastasis can now be detected in time through advanced technologies. 透過先進技術，癌細胞轉移可以被即時偵測。

❸ insomnia ▸ in（表否定）+ somn（睡眠）+ ia

n. 失眠

例：Taking sleeping pills would not cure your insomnia.
吃安眠藥並不會治好你的失眠。

❹ pneumonia ▸ pneumon（肺）+ ia

n. 肺炎

例：After suffering from pneumonia for one month, his health condition deteriorated. 在感染肺炎一個月後，他的健康狀況惡化了。

❺ homeostasis ▸ homeo（相同的）+ stasis

n. 體內平衡

例：Homeostasis represents the internal and physical stable conditions of our body. 體內平衡代表著我們身體內部和體能的穩定狀態。

Part1｜表示疾病、紀錄、學科、主義

graph、gram 紀錄

❶ choreography ▸ chor（舞蹈）+ eo + graphy

n. 編舞

例：The dance was a choreography by the award-winning Susan Stroman. 此舞蹈是由獲獎的蘇珊史托曼所編制。

❷ photograph ▸ photo（光）+ graph

n. 照片 v. 拍照

例：I took a random photograph of the couple at the corner and gave it to them. 我替站在街角的情侶隨機拍了一張照，並送給了他們。

❸ autograph ▸ auto（自我）+ graph

n./v. 親筆（簽名）

例：Mr. Hanks, can you kindly sigh me an autograph?
漢克斯先生，可以請你幫我簽名嗎？

❹ diagram ▸ dia（穿透）+ gram

n. 圖表

例：The diagram indicated that the user demographics is undergoing a major shift now. 此圖表顯示，用戶特徵正在歷經重大變動。

❺ program ▸ pro（向前的）+ gram

n. 計畫；程序表 v. 設計電腦程式

例：I guess I have to re-program the system to make it function again.
我想，為了要讓系統重新運作，我需要重新跑過程式。

Part1｜表示疾病、紀錄、學科、主義

logy 研究、學科

❶ astrology ▸ astro(star) + logy

n. 占星術（學）

例：Astrology is not only his hobby, but his expertise.
占星術不僅是他的興趣，還是他的專業。

❷ sociology ▸ soci(group) + o + logy

n. 社會學

例：Sociology aims to help people understand the patterns of societal relations and structures.
社會學旨在幫助人們瞭解社會關係和組織的模式。

❸ mythology ▸ myth（神話）+ ology

n. 神話學

例：Greek mythology is a required course in the Department of Foreign Languages and Literature. 希臘神話是外文系的必修科目。

❹ theology ▸ theo（神）+ logy

n. 神學

例：To understand the meanings of the Bible, studying theology may be helpful. 要了解聖經的意涵，修習神學也許會有幫助。

❺ biology ▸ bio（生物 = life）+ logy

n. 生物學

例：Among all the subjects, biology is my least favorite one.
在所有科目中，我最不喜歡的就是生物。

Part1 | 表示疾病、紀錄、學科、主義

phobia 恐懼症

❶ acrophobia ▶ acro（高處）+ phobia

n. 懼高症

例：Due to acrophobia, I rejected my friend's invitation to go bungee jumping. 因為懼高症，我拒絕我朋友去高空彈跳的邀約。

❷ hydrophobia ▶ hydro（水）+ phobia

n. 恐水症

例：My inherent hydrophobia deters me from doing all kinds of water sports. 我先天的恐水症讓我無法進行任何水上活動。

❸ claustrophobia ▶ claustro（關閉）+ phobia

n. 幽閉恐懼症

例：She has claustrophobia; that's why she gets nervous whenever she takes the elevator.
她有幽閉恐懼症，這是為什麼每當她搭電梯的時候都會變得緊張。

❹ xenophobia ▶ xeno（外來；陌生）+ phobia

n. 恐外症，對外國（人）的無理仇視或畏懼

例：Sadly, we are now facing the double phenomena of racism and xenophobia now.
令人難過的是，我們正面臨種族歧視和排外的雙重現象。

❺ nyctophobia ▶ nycto（夜晚）+ phobia

n. 黑夜恐懼症

例：My doctor said that nyctophobia may be the main cause for my insomnia. 我的醫生說，黑夜恐懼症可能是我失眠的主要原因。

mania 狂熱、病態

❶ bibliomania ▸ biblio（書）+ mania

n. 藏書癖；瘋狂愛書之人

例：Being a bibliomania means that I am inclined to spend a great sum of money on books. 當一名藏書癖代表我傾向於花大筆錢買書。

❷ egomania ▸ ego（自我）+ mania

n. 自大狂，利己者

例：Your excessive preference toward yourself has made you an utter egomania. 你對自我的極度偏好已經使你成為一個徹底的自大狂了。

❸ pyromania ▸ pyro（火）+ mania

n. 放火狂，縱火狂

例：The pyromania set fire on a building. Fortunately, it was abandoned and empty. 該名縱火狂放火燒了建物，好在其以廢棄空置。

❹ kleptomania ▸ kelpto（偷竊）+ mania

n. 竊盜癖

例：According to the article, there are different treatments for kleptomania. 根據文章，要治療竊盜癖有許多方法。

❺ trichotillomania ▸ tricho（毛髮 = hair）+ tillo（拉）+ mania

n. 拔毛症

例：The woman diagnosed with trichotillomania has pulled off all the hair on her body.
該名患有拔毛症的女子已經將其身上所有頭髮都拔掉了。

ism 行為、主義、學說

❶ heroism ▶ hero（英雄）+ ism

n. 英雄主義

例：Medieval heroism seems pretty outdated and unnecessary in modern times.
在當今社會中，中世紀式的英雄主義看來過時且不必要。

❷ alcoholism ▶ alcohol（酒精）+ ism

n. 酗酒

例：My uncle died of alcoholism and resultant complications.
我舅舅因酗酒和相關迸發症過世了。

❸ socialism ▶ social（社會的）+ ism

n. 社會主義

例：It seems like socialism has found its way back to this era.
看來，社會主義已悄悄在當今社會中回歸了。

❹ racism ▶ rac(e)（種族）+ ism

n. 種族歧視

例：We should stand up for our own rights and fight racism.
我們應捍衛自己的權利，對抗種族歧視。

❺ terrorism ▶ terror（恐怖）+ ism

n. 恐怖主義

例：Let's hope no acts of terrorism like 911 ever happen again.
讓我們祈禱像911 事件的恐怖攻擊不會再次發生。

Part1 | 表示疾病、紀錄、學科、主義

ics 學科、學術

❶ athletics ▶ athlet（運動）+ ics

n. 體育運動，競技

例：The athletics competition is soon to be held in this stadium.
運動競賽很快就會在此體育館舉行。

❷ economics ▶ eco（住所）+ nom（法令）+ ics

n. 經濟、經濟學

例：A good command of economics is essential to be a competent minister of economic affairs. 熟稔經濟學是勝任經濟部長的重要條件。

❸ electronics ▶ electron（電子）+ ics

n. 電子學

例：Now, the electronics industry is facing an unprecedented crisis.
現在，電子產業正面臨前所未有的危機。

❹ mechanics ▶ mechan（機器）+ ics

n. 力學，機械學，運作方式

例：You need to master the principles of the mechanics of this system before using it. 在使用前，你必須先懂得此系統的運作方式。

❺ aesthetics ▶ aesthe（感覺）+ ics

n. 美學

例：The sensibility of aesthetics is vanishing in the fast-faced technological era. 美學感知力正在快速進展的科技時代中消逝。

Part2｜表示職業、身份、性別、地點

arian ……類型的人

❶ humanitarian ▸ human（人）+ it + arian

n. 人道主義者

例：Several countries are asking for humanitarian aids now.
現在許多國家正在群求人道援助。

❷ vegetarian ▸ veget（蔬菜）+ arian

n. 素食者

例：Living a life as a vegetarian actually fulfills her on a spiritual level.
以吃素的方式生活讓她感到精神層次上的富足。

❸ barbarian ▸ barbar（古怪的；野蠻）+ arian

n. 野蠻人

例：He's such a barbarian that he says and does rude things to others.
他真是個野蠻人，對他人説無禮的話、做無禮的事。

❹ librarian ▸ libr（書）+ arian

n. 圖書館員

例：Working as a librarian is my lifetime dream.
當名圖書館員是我畢生的夢想。

❺ plasticarian ▸ plastic（塑膠）+ arain

n. 不使用塑膠的人

例：My sister is a hardcore plasticarian – she even scolds others for using plastic products.
我妹妹強烈堅持不用塑膠，她甚至會責罵使用塑膠產品的人。

Part2｜表示職業、身份、性別、地點

dom 地方、領域、狀態、身份

❶ kingdom ▶ king（國王）+ dom

n. 王國

例：The princess lives in a fairy kingdom with no worries.
公主毫無憂慮地在奇幻王國中生活。

❷ freedom ▶ free（自由的）+ dom

n. 自由

例：The freedom of speech should be granted to all people.
人人皆應擁有言論自由。

❸ wisdom ▶ wis(e)（有智慧的）+ dom

n. 智慧，明智，知識

例：These brewing techniques are ancient wisdoms; we should pass them on. 此釀造技巧是先人智慧，我們應使其流傳下去。

❹ stardom ▶ star（明星）+ dom

n. 演員的身分，明星地位，演藝圈

例：The young actress rose to stardom after the release of the blockbuster. 年輕女演員在電影賣座後成為明星。

❺ officialdom ▶ official（官方的）+ dom

n. 官場，官僚主義，官員

例：The officialdom has already consumed too much of our energy.
官僚主義已經消耗掉我們太多精力了。

Part2｜表示職業、身份、性別、地點

um 地方

❶ stadium ▶ sta（站立= stand）+ di + um

n. 體育場，運動場

例：The stadium was already packed with people for Super Bowl's Half-time Show. 為了觀賞超級盃的半場秀，體育館早擠滿了人。

❷ auditorium ▶ audit（聽）+ orium

n. 禮堂，會堂

例：Haven't you heard that the location of the ceremony was changed to the auditorium? 你沒聽說儀式的地點被改至禮堂了嗎？

❸ aquarium ▶ aqua（水）+ ium

n. 水族館

例：I love marine animals, and I think the new aquarium is a perfect place for our trip. 我喜歡海洋生物，我認為新的水族館會是很好的旅遊地點。

❹ planetarium ▶ plant（行星）+ arium

n. 天文館

例：The planetarium opens from 9 a.m. to 10 p.m.
此天文館從早上九點開放至晚上十點。

❺ symposium ▶ sym（一起= together）+ pos(is)（喝）+ ium

n. 討論會；座談會

例：The theme of this year's symposium is the idea of democracy in the era of fake news. 今年座談會的主題是假訊息時代中的民主概念。

Part3｜表示性質、特質

ship
狀態、身分、關係

❶ scholarship ▸ scholar（學術）+ ship

n. 獎學金；學術成就

例：After months of waiting, I finally got the acceptance letter and the scholarship. 在等待數個月後，我終於收到了入學通知和獎學金。

❷ friendship ▸ friend（朋友）+ ship n. 友誼

例：Building a healthy friendship takes practices and patience.
建立健康的友誼需要練習和耐心。

❸ ownership ▸ owner（所有人）+ ship

n. 物主身分

例：Can you help to look up the ownership of this purse?
你可以幫我查詢這個包包的主人是誰嗎？

❹ apprenticeship ▸ apprentice（學徒）+ ship

n. 學徒身分，學徒期間

例：After serving my apprenticeship with my father, I opened my own factory now. 在擔任我爸爸的學徒之後，我現在開了自己的工廠。

❺ citizenship ▸ citizen（公民）+ ship

n. 公民權，公民身份，公民義務

例：Being born in Taiwan doesn't mean you have Taiwanese citizenship.
在台灣出生不代表擁有台灣公民身份。

Part 4｜表示狀態、情況

ee、eer、er、or
從事……的人、做……動作者

❶ employee ▸ employ（雇用）+ ee

n. 受僱者，員工

例：All the employees resigned at once because of repetitive delayed salaries. 因持續延遲發薪，所有的員工同時辭職。

❷ refugee ▸ refug(e)（避難）+ ee

n. 難民，流亡者

例：The refugees traveled hundreds of miles just to find a safe place to rest. 難民跋涉百哩，只為了找到棲身之所。

❸ volunteer ▸ volunt（意志）+ eer

n. 志工，志願者

例：The organization was recruiting volunteers to help the pharmacists now. 該組織正招募員工幫助藥劑師。

❹ admirer ▸ admir(e)（讚賞）+ er

n. 讚賞者，愛慕者

例：The tarot cards read that you now have several admirers.
根據塔羅牌，你現在有好幾個愛慕者。

❺ mentor ▸ ment（心智）+ or

n. 導師，恩師 v. 指導

例：If I hadn't met my mentor, I wouldn't have chosen literature as my major. 如果我沒有遇見我的恩師，我當初不會選擇文學當作主修。

Part 4｜表示狀態、情況

ess 女性身份

❶ actress ▸ act（演戲）+ r + ess

n. 女性演員

例：The actress delivered a moving acceptance speech in the award ceremony. 在頒獎典禮中，女演員發表了一場動人的得獎演說。

❷ goddess ▸ god（神）+ d + ess

n. 女神

例：Athena is the goddess of victory in Greek mythology.
在希臘神話中，雅典娜是勝利女人。

❸ heiress ▸ heir（繼承人）+ ess

n. 女性的繼承人

例：I'm the only heiress to my father's mansion and the farmland.
我是我父親豪宅和農地的唯一女繼承人。

❹ hostess ▸ host（主人）+ ess

n. 女主人

例：The host and the hostess greeted us with a warm welcome.
男主人和女主人熱情歡迎及招待我們。

❺ princess ▸ princ(e)（王子）+ ess

n. 公主

例：To dream of living like a princess will make you an impractical person. 想像過著公主般的生活會讓你變得不切實際。

hood 身分、時期

❶ childhood ▶ child（孩童）+ hood

n. 童年

例：My traumatic childhood induce to my insecurities and fear of intimacy. 我的創傷童年導致我的不安全感以及對親密性的恐懼。

❷ falsehood ▶ false（虛假的）+ hood

n. 虛假，謊言

例：Falsehoods about the disease may lead to unnecessary social panic. 關於該疫情的留言可能對導致不必要的大眾恐慌。

❸ likelihood ▶ likel(y)（可能的）+ i + hood

n. 可能性

例：The likelihood of winning the lottery is extremely low.
中樂透的可能性非常低。

❹ parenthood ▶ parent（父母）+ hood

n. 父母身分

例：Entering parenthood lays enormous pressure on my sister.
準備要為人母讓我姊姊承受巨大壓力。

❺ brotherhood ▶ brother（兄弟）+ hood

n. 手足之情，兄弟關係（情誼）

例：A strong bond of brotherhood kept us together during tough times.
強烈的兄弟情誼讓我們在艱難時刻相互扶持。

Part 4｜表示狀態、情況

ian、ist 從事……者、某主義或信仰的遵守者

❶ musician ▶ music（音樂）+ ian

n. 音樂家，樂手

例：My father used to be in a famous jazz band of 8 musicians.
我爸爸曾經加入過一個八人的知名爵士樂團。

❷ politician ▶ politc(s)（政治）+ ian n. 政治人物

例：That politician was validating his own existence again.
該名政客又再刷存在感了。

❸ guardian ▶ gaurd（守護）+ ian

n. 監護人，守護者，管理員

例：After my sister passed away, I decided to become her children's legal guardian. 我姊姊過世後，我決定成為她小孩的法定監護人。

❹ psychologist ▶ psycho（心理）+ logist

n. 心理學家

例：The prestigious psychologist claimed that such a policy can actually make some deterrent effects.
該名具有聲望的心理學家表示，此政策可預期達到遏止效果。

❺ terrorist ▶ terror（恐怖）+ ist n. 恐怖分子

例：The government finally captured the infamous terrorists and put them into jail. 政府終於將惡名昭彰的恐怖份子逮捕入獄。

Part 4｜表示狀態、情況

ous 充滿……的

❶ various ▸ var（改變）+ ious

adj. 多種的，多樣的，形形色色的

例：There are various kinds of cosmetics for you to choose from.
這裡有多種化妝品任你挑選。

❷ victorious ▸ victor(y)（勝利）+ ious

adj. 勝利的，獲勝的

例：The victorious smile on her smile made all of us proud.
她臉上露出的勝利笑容使我們都感到驕傲。

❸ virtuous ▸ virtu(e)（美德）+ ious

adj. 有道德的，正直的

例：A virtuous man sticks to moral principles and his conscience.
一個正直的人會堅守道德規則和其良知。

❹ conscious ▸ con（一起）+ sci（知道 = know）+ ous

adj. 有意識的

例：The man was conscious now, so the investigation resumed.
男子恢復意識了，所以調查繼續進行。

❺ spacious ▸ spac(e)（空間）+ ious

adj. 寬敞的

例：The spacious living room elevates the whole visual experience.
這個寬敞的客廳提升了整體的視覺經驗。

Part 4｜表示狀態、情況

able、ible 可以……的

❶ traceable ▸ trace（痕跡）+ able

adj. 可追蹤的，可追溯的

例：The footprints of the wolf were barely traceable. We've lost track.
狼的足跡幾乎難以追蹤，我們沒有線索了。

❷ breakable ▸ break（打破）+ able

adj. 會破裂的 n. 易碎物

例：This item is highly breakable and needs extra wrapping.
這個產品非常易碎，需要額外包裝。

❸ changeable ▸ change（改變）+ able

adj. 可改變的，易變的

例：The weather is quite changeable in the mountain.
山上的天氣變化多端。

❹ tangible ▸ tang（接觸 = touch）+ ible

adj. 可觸的，實體的

例：Air and light are intangible, while the table you write on is tangible.
空氣和光是摸不到的，但是你寫作的桌子就是實體的。

❺ edible ▸ ed（吃 = eat）+ ible

adj. 可食用的

例：This product is not edible, and you should keep it out of children's reach. 這個產品不能吃，你要放在小孩碰不到的地方。

Part 4 | 表示狀態、情況

ive 有……傾向的、有……性質的

❶ creative ▶ creat(e)（創造）+ ive

adj. 創造（性）的

例：I took Creative Writing in the English Department this semester.
我這學期在英語系修了創意寫作。

❷ conclusive ▶ conclu(de)（結論）+ sive

adj. 決定性的，最終的

例：The decision is conclusive, and I hope there are no objections.
這是最終決定，我希望沒有反對意見。

❸ native ▶ nat（出生=born）+ ive

adj. 天生的；本地的

例：This fruit is native to Taichung and has been sold to many South Asian countries. 這是台中產的水果，且已銷往許多東南亞國家。

❹ pervasive ▶ per（徹底的=through）+ va(de)（走 = walk）+ sive

adj. 普遍的，滲透蔓延的

例：The film's pervasive violence upset many parents.
這部電影裡大量的暴力讓許多家長感到不滿。

❺ operative ▶ operat(e)（操作）+ ive

adj. 操作的，運作的 n. 技工

例：The operative procedure of the machine is written on the board.
機器的操作流程已經寫在板子上了。

Part 4｜表示狀態、情況

ern、ward 在……方向的

❶ western ▶ west（西方）+ ern

adj. 西方的；向西的

例：Western civilization still has a huge impact in Asia.
西方文明對亞洲仍有很大的影響。

❷ southern ▶ south（南方）+ ern

adj. 南方的；向南的

例：People from the southern part of the country are generally more easy-going. 這個國家的南部人通常都比較好相處。

❸ eastward ▶ east（東方）+ ward

adj./adv. 向東的（地）

例：Let's head eastward and appreciate the grand canyon.
我們往東邊走，欣賞大峽谷吧！

❹ wayward ▶ way（方向）+ ward

adj. 任性的，不規則的

例：His wayward personality makes him difficult to get along with.
他任性的性格讓他很難相處。

❺ homeward ▶ home（家）+ ward

adj./adv. 往家的方向的（地）

例：On the homeward train, I got really nostalgic and teary.
在往家的火車上，我變得很思鄉，淚眼汪汪。

Part 4｜表示狀態、情況

some
有……性質的

❶ awesome ▸ awe（敬畏）+ some

adj. 令人驚嘆的，絕佳的

例：Your speech was just awesome and mind-blowing!
你的演說真是精彩且令人讚嘆！

❷ tiresome ▸ tire（疲倦）+ some adj. 令人疲倦的

例：After the tiresome journey, I fell asleep in seconds.
在令人疲累的旅途之後，我很快就睡著了。

❸ troublesome ▸ trouble（麻煩）+ some

adj. 麻煩的

例：The project is troublesome and time-consuming; I think I need a hand. 這個企劃很麻煩且耗時。我覺得我需要幫忙。

❹ loathsome ▸ loath（厭惡）+ some

adj. 令人討厭的

例：On the contrary, human beings are the most loathsome creature on earth. 相反來說，人類才是地球上最令人討厭的生物。

❺ lonesome ▸ lone（獨自的）+ some

adj. 寂寞的，荒涼的

例：On a lonesome night, he drank up a bottle of whiskey.
在獨自一人的夜晚，他喝掉了整瓶威士忌。

Part 4｜表示狀態、情況

way、wise 在……方面的

❶ midway ▸ mid（中間的）+ way

adj./adv. 中途的（地），中間的（地）

例：I prefer to sit in a midway position when going to the movie theater.
去電影院看電影時，我偏好坐在中間的位置。

❷ seaway ▸ sea（海）+ way

n. 海上航道

例：Please show me the seaway bill before you proceed to the next step. 在進行下一個步驟前，請給我看海運單。

❸ counterclockwise

▸ counter（反抗 = against）+ clockwise（順時針的）

adj. 逆時針方向的

例：How come the minute hand goes clockwise and the second hand goes counterclockwise?
為什麼分針往順時針方向走，秒針卻往逆時針方向走？

❹ budget-wise ▸ budget（預算）+ wise

adj. 預算方面的

例：Well, budget-wise, it is barely enough to implement a project this scale. 這個嘛，就預算來說，根本不夠實行這種規模的專案。

❺ weather-wise ▸ weather（天氣）+ wise

adj. 天氣方面的

例：It's a perfect day for hiking, weather-wise.
就天氣方面來看，今天很適合去爬山。

Part 4 | 表示狀態、情況

less 不能……的、沒有……的

❶ priceless ▶ price（價格）+ less

adj. 貴重的，無價的

例：A person's genuine kindness is rare and priceless.
一個人真誠的善意是罕見且無價的。

❷ careless ▶ care（注意）+ less

adj. 粗心的，草率的

例：A careless mistake can sometimes lead to major disasters.
一個粗心的錯誤有時候可能會導致重大災難。

❸ dauntless ▶ daunt（畏懼）+ less

adj. 無懼的，大膽的

例：His dauntless spirit encouraged the team and achieved a great success. 他無所畏懼的精神鼓舞了團隊，達到極大的成功。

❹ countless ▶ count（數量）+ less

adj. 無數的，數不盡的

例：Why do you always have countless excuses to evade the problem?
你怎麼總是有數不完的藉口來逃避問題？

❺ ceaseless ▶ cease（停止）+ less

adj. 不間斷的

例：The ceaseless war had turn people's life into a living hell.
連續不停的戰爭已經讓人民的生活變成人間煉獄。

let、ling、ule 小的

❶ booklet ▶ book（書）+ let

n. 小冊子

例：The design of the endpapers on the booklet were surprisingly exquisite. 令人驚喜的是，小冊子上卷首和卷尾的空頁設計相當精美。

❷ leaflet ▶ leaf（葉子）+ let

n. 傳單；小葉子

例：The leaflet reads that the band is having a gig in a park.
傳單上說，樂團要在公園舉行小演出。

❸ duckling ▶ duck（鴨子）+ ling

n. 小鴨

例：Ugly Duckling is a well-known fable by Hans Christian Anderson.
醜小鴨是安徒生所寫的著名寓言故事。

❹ sibling ▶ sib（血親）+ ling

n. 兄弟姊妹

例：I have five siblings, and we all have distinctive personalities.
我有五個兄弟姊妹，我們每個人的個性都很獨特。

❺ granule ▶ gran（顆粒）+ ule

n. 細粒，顆粒

例：I have only a granule of bread left to feed my guinea pig.
我只剩一小粒麵包給我的天竺鼠吃。

fy 表示……動作的

❶ clarify ▶ clar（清楚的）+ i + fy

V. 澄清，闡明

例：Let me clarify: this article is formulated to protect the minorities.
讓我澄清一下：此法條是制定用來保護弱勢族群的。

❷ purify ▶ pur(e)（純淨的）+ fy

V. 淨化，使純淨

例：The reason why I enjoy hiking is that mountain scenes purify my thoughts. 我喜歡爬山的原因是因為山景能淨化我的思緒。

❸ classify ▶ class（階級）+ i + fy

V. 分類

例：Please classify the files in either a chronological or alphabetical order. 請將檔案用時間順序或是字母開頭分類好。

❹ beautify ▶ beaut（美麗）+ i + fy

V. 美化

例：The oil painting surely beautify the master bedroom.
此油畫確實讓主臥房看起來更賞心悅目了。

❺ specify ▶ spec(t)（看= look）+ i + fy

V. 具體說明，詳細說明

例：The interviewer asked me to specify my thesis statement in five minutes. 面試官要求我在五分鐘內具體解釋我的主題論述。

Part 4｜表示狀態、情況

ish、like 像……般的

❶ selfish ▸ self（自我）+ ish

adj. 自私的

例：His selfish demeanor irritated everyone at present.
他自私的舉動激怒了在場所有人。

❷ foolish ▸ fool（愚笨的人）+ ish

adj. 愚蠢的，愚笨的

例：Such a foolish act may cost your life!
如此愚蠢的行為可能會使你喪命！

❸ boyish ▸ boy（男孩）+ like

adj. 男孩子氣的，像小男孩一般的

例：The boyish dressing style is popular among young and old alike now. 男孩子氣的穿衣風格現在很受男女老少歡迎。

❹ dreamlike ▸ dream（夢）+ like

adj. 如夢一般的

例：The dreamlike chance encounter reminded me of my first love.
如夢一般的偶遇讓我想到了我的初戀。

❺ childlike ▸ child（小孩的）+ like

adj. 孩子氣的

例：I want to get rid of my childlike and immature temperament.
我想要擺脱我小孩子氣和不成熟的個性。

Part 4｜表示狀態、情況

ility 具有……性質、可……性

❶ unpredictability ▶ un（表否定）+ pre（先前）+ dict（說）+ abl(e)（可以的）+ ility

n. 無法預期性

例：The unpredictability of the formula made the system unstable.
此公式的不可預期性讓系統變的不穩定。

❷ mobility ▶ mobil(e)（流動的）+ ility

n. 流動性，移動性，機動性

例：The serious illness limits the man's mobility for a long time.
身患重病限制了男子的行動力好長一段時間。

❸ usability ▶ us(e)（使用）+ abl(e)（可以的）+ ility

n. 可用性

例：This equipment has no usability whatsoever and should be eliminated. 這個設備一點用處都沒有，應該被淘汰。

❹ visibility ▶ vis（看見）+ ibl(e)（可以的）+ ility

n. 能見度

例：The low visibility in the mist made driving highly dangerous.
霧中的能見度很低，開車變得相當危險。

❺ eligibility ▶ e + lig（選擇）+ ibl(e)（可以的）+ ility

n. 資格；適任

例：I hope I can acquire the eligibility to run for the President.
我希望我能得到選總統的資格。

Part 4｜表示狀態、情況

ade 行為、人、集體

❶ parade ▸ par（準備）+ ade

n. 遊行

例：Tons of people gathered in the square for the annual parade.
許多人聚集在廣場準備參加年度遊行。

❷ lemonade ▸ lemon（檸檬）+ ade

n. 檸檬水

例：Many children will go on the street and sell lemonade for fun.
許多小孩會上街賣檸檬水當作娛樂。

❸ blockade ▸ block（阻礙）+ ade

n. 封鎖，障礙（物） v. 封鎖，阻礙

例：The heavy traffic flow was a blockade for us to run a smooth demonstration. 交通阻塞阻礙我們舉行一場流動順暢的遊行。

❹ renegade ▸ reneg(e)（背信）+ ade

n. 叛徒，背信者 adj. 背信的 v. 背叛，背信

例：Having different faiths from yours doesn't make me a renegade.
和你們的信念不同，不代表我就是個叛徒。

❺ masquerade ▸ masque（面具）+ er（表人）+ ade

n. 化裝舞會

例：Romeo and Juliet met in a masquerade and soon fell in love.
羅密歐和茱麗葉是在一場化妝舞會認識的，且快速墜入愛河。

tion、sion 行動、狀態

❶ persuasion ▸ persua(de)（說服）+ sion

n. 說服（力），勸服

例：Her excellent powers of persuasion led the team to success in the debate. 她高超的遊說能力帶領團隊在辯論中得到勝利。

❷ donation ▸ don（給予）+ ation

n. 贊助，捐贈

例：The organization received a donation of 1 million dollars last night. 組織昨晚收到了一筆一百萬的贊助。

❸ realization ▸ realiz(e)（理解）+ ation

n. 領悟；體現

例：I suddenly had a realization that we need to love ourselves first. 我突然間頓悟到，我們應該要先愛自己。

❹ confrontation ▸ con（共同）+ front（正面的）+ ation

n. 對抗

例：The fierce confrontation surprisingly ended up in a mutual reconciliation. 令人驚奇的是，激烈的對抗最後竟變成雙方和解。

❺ tension ▸ tens（拉）+ ion

n. 緊張、緊繃

例：The tension between them somehow disturbed all of us. 他們之間的緊繃關係讓我們所有人感到不安。

Part 4 | 表示狀態、情況

ance、ancy、ence、ency 性質、狀態

❶ assistance ▶ assist（協助）+ ance

n. 幫助，援助

例：Your financial assistance comes just in time. 你的金援來的正是時候。

❷ infancy ▶ infan(t)（嬰兒）+ cy

n. 嬰兒期，發展階段

例：During infancy, sufficient nutrition is critical in the overall development.
在嬰兒期的時候，充足的影響對整體生長來說至關重要。

❸ vacancy ▶ vac（空的）+ ancy

n. 空缺，空白，空地，空房

例：There's only one vacancy left for the position. Grab your chance!
這個職缺只剩下一個名額。把握機會！

❹ excellence ▶ excel（勝出）+ ence

n. 傑出，卓越

例：His excellence in architecture won him both money and fame.
他在建築上的卓越表現贏得他財富和名聲。

❺ emergency ▶ e（向外= out）+ merg（沉沒 = sink）+ ency

n. 緊急情況

例：You can only call this number under emergency.
你只有在緊急情況下才能打這個號碼。

Part 4｜表示狀態、情況

age 狀況、行為、集合、性質

❶ shortage ▸ short（少的）+ age

n. 不足，缺少

例：The shortage of budget has put the company in a dire situation now. 預算不足讓公司陷入急迫的處境。

❷ homage ▸ hom（人= man）+ age

n. 敬意，尊敬

例：Many fans from all over the world came to pay homage to the actress. 許多來自世界各地的粉絲來向女明星表示敬意。

❸ mileage ▸ mile（公里）+ age

n. 里程數

例：The mileage on the odometer showed that you need to buy a new car. 里程表上的里程數顯示你該買一台新車了。

❹ storage ▸ stor(e)（儲存）+ age

n. 貯藏（量），庫存

例：The storage room is large enough to contain hundreds of products. 倉庫大到可以儲放上百件商品。

❺ breakage ▸ break（破壞）+ age

n. 壞損，破損

例：The accidental breakage of the vase led to a loss of a 1-million-dollar order. 花瓶意外破損讓我們損失了一筆一百萬元的訂單。

Part 4｜表示狀態、情況

ment 行為、行動

❶ movement ▸ move（移動）+ ment

n. 動作，行動，（政治、社會、思想）運動

例：The lady's slow movement hinted that her left foot was hurt.
女子緩慢的動作暗示著她的左腳受傷了。

❷ resentment ▸ re（再次 = again）+ sent（情感）+ ment

n. 仇恨，怨恨

例：I don't harbor resentment. Let bygones be bygones.
我心中沒有仇恨。過去的就讓它過去。

❸ encouragement ▸ en（使）+ courage（勇氣）+ ment

n. 鼓勵，促進，激勵

例：My professor's encouragement truly motivated me to study harder.
我的教授對我的鼓勵真的成為我更努力讀書的動力。

❹ arrangement ▸ arrange（安排）+ ment

n. 安排，行前準備，排列

例：Can you make some arrangements for the meeting on Friday?
你可以替週五的會議做點安排嗎？

❺ payment ▸ pay（付費）+ ment

n. 付款，支付，款項

例：Delayed payment is unacceptable and against the law based on the contract. 延遲付款是無法被接受的，且根據合約是違法的。

NOTE

Test

綜合測驗

— TEST —
綜合測驗

一、看字根/字首/字尾猜意思

(　　) 1. mis-

A. 錯誤的　B. 一半　C. 反對　D. 分離；離開

(　　) 2. fin

A. 個人　B. 步伐　C. 重的　D. 限制、界限

(　　) 3. homo-

A. 生命、生物　B. 一起　C. 相同的　D. 表否定

(　　) 4. civi

A. 公民　B. 身體　C. 睡眠　D. 手

(　　) 5. ex-

A. 超過　B. 向外；之前的　C. 穿越　D. 做

(　　) 6. cide

A. 殺　B. 交叉　C. 耕種　D. 分離；離開

(　　) 7. grav

A. 大的　B. 小的　C. 重的　D. 性質、狀態

(　　) 8. ous

A. 快樂　B. 充滿……的　C. 表示……動作的　D. 可以……的

(　　) 9. center, centr

A. 可以……的　B. 中心　C. 反對　D. 表示……動作的

(　　) 10. chron

A. 數字　B. 跟隨　C. 測量　D. 時間

(　　) 11. press

A. 神經　B. 人類　C. 壓　D. 推

(　　) 12. spect

A. 符號　B. 運送　C. 掛　D. 看

(　　) 13. tri-

A. 三　B. 四　C. 五　D. 七

(　　) 14. un-

A. 快樂　B. 傷心　C. 表否定　D. 表肯定

(　　) 15. mal-

A. 好的　B. 惡的　C. 假的　D. 不同的

(　　) 16. counter-

A. 吃　B. 說話　C. 反對、阻抗　D. 再次

(　　) 17. log, loq

A. 透過　B. 軍事　C. 說話　D. 自我

(　　) 18. psych

A. 生命　B. 群體　C. 心理、精神　D. 自我

(　　) 19. demo

A. 政府　B. 心　C. 皮膚　D. 人民

(　　) 20. aqua

A. 火　B. 水　C. 土地　D. 星

解答： 1. A 2. D 3. C 4. A 5. B　6. A 7. C 8. B 9. B 10. D
11. C 12. D 13. A 14. C 15. B　16. C 17. C 18. C 19. D 20. B

二、下列例句均取自書中，請寫出底線處代表的意思。

_______1. The memorial park and the bar are only two miles a**part**.

_______2. The tests for coronavirus were **neg**ative. What a great relief.

_______3. The government invested billions of US dollars to build this giant **aero**plane.

_______4. Sex before marriage is considered **im**pure by many Christians.

_______5. This medicine is going to **bene**fit you in the long term.

_______6. This is not **pseudo**science. It has solid proof.

_______7. Take her onto the **ambul**ance for emergency treatment!

_______8. The politician **claim**ed that he was wronged by the allegation.

_______9. The enemy certainly out**number**ed us in this battle.

_______10. Today is my parent's 20th **ann**iversary.

解答：1.部分　2.否定　3.空氣　4.否定　5.好的
6.假的　7.走　8.喊　9.數字　10. 年

三、依據上下文意思，試填入正確的選項。

① Danny is a crazy about science. He loves to ______ new things. However, he is only a _____, namely, not familiar with many procedures. He had ______ to become a great scientist when he was little.

② It it no doubt that elders need extra care. They may need ______ from others in order to accomplish daily activities. However, if being _____, terrible _____ may occur.

A. create	**B. decided**	**C. assitance**
D. neglected	**E. novice**	**F. accident**

解答：① AEB　② CDF

中譯：A. 創造　B. 決定　C. 幫助

D. 忽視、忽略　E. 初學者、新手　F. 意外、偶發事件

四、下列例句均取自書中，請寫出底線處代表的意思。

(　　) 1. I cannot ______ such rudeness.

A. suffer　B. refer　C. defer　D. transfer

(　　) 2. I was _______ to finish the paper before the deadline.

A. unaware　B. uncertain　C. unable　D. unhappy

(　　) 3. This ________ software can protect your computer.

A. antiwar　B. antivirus　C. anti-aging　D. antibody

(　　) 4. A lot of my classmates were ______ today.

A. abrupt　B. absent　C. abduct　D. abnormal

(　　) 5. The film temporarily _______ me from all the nuisance.

A. distracted　B. distributed　C. disregarded　D. dishonest

(　　) 6. She couldn't _________ on a book very long.

A. eccentric　B. Epicenter　C. concentrate　D. centralize

(　　) 7. I'm dying to see the ______ of the film!

A. consequent　B. prosecute　C. sequel　D. subsequent

(　　) 8. Many people seek ______ by buying lots of high-end products.

A. discomfort　B. effort　C. fortitude　D. comfort

(　　) 9. Show some _______ to your parents and behave!

A. respect　B. prospect　C. suspect　D. expect

(　　)10. This presentation _______ of three main parts.

A. assisted　B. consisted　C. insisted　D. persisted

(　　)11. Our goal is to ______ this aim that everyone gets a mask to wear everyday.

A. tenacious　B. attain　C. continue　D. contain

(　　)12. I _____ a great sense of satisfaction by helping others.

A. entertain　B. maintain　C. obtain　D. sustain

解答：1. A 我不能**容忍**這種粗魯的舉止。　2. C 我**無法**在期限之前寫完報告。　3. B 這個**防毒**軟體可以防護你的電腦。　4. B 今天我很多同學**缺席**。　5. A 這部電影短暫地使我能夠**分心**，不去想所有煩心的事。　6. C 她不能長時間**專心**讀一本書。　7. C 我等不及要看這部電影的**續集**。　8. D 許多人透過購買高檔產品來尋求**慰藉**。　9. A **尊重**你的父母，注意你的行為！　10. B 這份報告由三個部分**組成**。　11. B 我們的目標是**達到**每個人每天都有口罩可以帶。　12. C 透過幫助別人，我**得到**很大的滿足感。

五、填空式翻譯

1. They were charged with ____________ the public peace.
 他們被指控擾亂公共治安。

2. The team won consecutive _________ in the championship!
 該隊在錦標賽中獲得連勝！

3. Both of my grandparents are _____________ and I wish to become one in the future.
 我的祖父母們都是生物學家，我希望我未來也是。

4. I usually get quite ______________ before making a public speech.
 在演講之前，我總是會變得非常緊張。

5. He listened to the speech with ___________and left right after it ended.

他漠不關心地聽著演講，並在結束後馬上離去。

6. Keeping a work-life bablance is ___________.

維持工作與生活平衡是極其重要的。

解答： 1:disturbing　2. victories　3. biologists
4. nervous　5. apathy　6. vital

六、整句式翻譯

1. 我們有時會違背自己的意願去做某些事情，就只為了要取悅朋友。

（109 學測）

2. 隨著世界人口持續增加，各國正以不同的速度失去土壤。

（108 統測）

參考解答：

1.Sometimes, we might go against our will to do things to make our friends happy.

2.As the world's population continues to increase, countries are losing their soil with different speed.

原來如此 系列 E231

破解英文單字：字首×字根×字尾這樣用

聽明學習英文單字記憶訣竅，事半功倍就用字首字根字尾

作　　者　許豪 ◎著
顧　　問　曾文旭
社　　長　王毓芳
編輯統籌　耿文國、黃璽宇
主　　編　吳靜宜、姜怡安
執行編輯　吳佳芬
美術編輯　王桂芳、張嘉容
封面設計　阿作
法律顧問　北辰著作權事務所　蕭雄淋律師、幸秋妙律師

初　　版　2020年08月
出　　版　捷徑文化出版事業有限公司
電　　話　（02）2752-5618
傳　　真　（02）2752-5619

定　　價　新台幣320元／港幣107元
產品內容　1書

總 經 銷　采舍國際有限公司
地　　址　235 新北市中和區中山路二段366巷10號3樓
電　　話　（02）8245-8786
傳　　真　（02）8245-8718

港澳地區總經銷　和平圖書有限公司
地　　址　香港柴灣嘉業街12號百樂門大廈17樓
電　　話　（852）2804-6687
傳　　真　（852）2804-6409

▶本書部分圖片由 Shutterstock、freepik 圖庫提供。

國家圖書館出版品預行編目資料

破解英文單字：字首×字根×字尾這樣用／
許豪著. -- 初版. -- 臺北市：捷徑文化, 2020.08
　面；　公分. -- (原來如此；E231)

ISBN 978-986-5507-31-2(平裝)

1. 英語　2. 詞彙

805.12　　109009437